double trouble

When **LIFE** gives you **LEMONS**

Squirt someone in the eye with them.

Leaving St. Louis (Hour of the Late-Night Greyhound Station)

It was just past midnight and I was trudging through the St. Louis Greyhound station, a grim building obviously brought to you by the people who design high school bathrooms. I had spent two and a half days on the bus to get here, and now, after only a few hours in St. Louis, I was about to spend another two and a half days getting home to San Francisco. My hair smelled like diesel fuel and my teeth felt as if they were covered in Greyhound upholstery. But the fighting spirit of the Vickers clan means we never give up. We just whine to our friends.

I flipped open my cell phone and called my best buddy, Emma, for the ninth time in the last hour. For the ninth time I got to listen to her voicemail message.

"I'm sorry, Emma's answering machine is broken. This is her refrigerator. Please leave your _____ of the beep, and I will stick it to myself with _____

"Hey there, this is Cathy. Answer your phone before I blow it up with my telepathic death rays." I snapped the phone shut and stuffed it back into my pocket.

How I Spent My Summer Vacation (Hour of the Recap)

It had been six months since I found out my boyfriend, Victor, was immortal. Yes, immortal: as in, the owner of a literally perfect body; strong, fast, and more than a little hot, which a young man ought to be if he can possibly manage it. I had seen Victor, riddled with bullet holes, heal in front of my eyes. It sounds great, I know—who hasn't wanted a boyfriend you could push in front of a bus with no lasting consequences?—but in practice it didn't do me any good because I never got to see the guy. He was currently locked in a secret lab somewhere working two jobs—"principal scientist" and "number one guinea pig"—trying to discover the biochemical secrets of immortality. This was severely cutting into our quality time.

Beyond my elusive boyfriend, it had been six weeks since I graduated from high school with no measurable job skills, unless Advanced Doodling counts. To my amazement, my mother's gloomy assessment of the job market for eighteen-year-old cartoonists with short attention spans appeared to be fairly accurate, and I had been getting fired from roughly one crappy entry-level job per week since school got out.

Q: Cathy, why did you take a Greyhound to St. Louis in the first place?

2.

A: To see an immortal fortune-teller named Auntie Joe. Aren't you glad you asked?

About Immortals

They exist. For the most part, they blend in, except they tend to have a little extra spending money on account of having a jillion years to fatten their savings accounts without spending a penny on life insurance.

According to Victor, immortals don't know they are immortal until the moment they should have died. Something about the near-death experience seems to flip the switch on the immortality gene. Victor had been twenty-two when he was trapped in the mining accident that should have killed him. Now he would be twenty-two forever.

About Auntie Joe

At the end of my last set of adventures, I got a mysterious package with a St. Louis phone number on the shipping label. When I called the number, I found it led to a website with a message just for me. It was about an immortal named Tsao, who had been haunting me for the last six months, inviting me to dinner, dropping by my house, and making excuses to be alone with me. The message was a story about the last days before Tsao had become immortal, a thousand years ago. Here's the business end of the story:

> *...Now it chanced that in the royal city at that time there lived a young woman of great spirit born on the first day of the year*

www.luckyfortuneforyou.com/cathy.html

of the Fire Tiger. Tsao saw her one day in the marketplace, and her glance passed through his heart like an arrow: the breath and life struck from him in an instant, and the sound of the bowstring still humming.

He pursued the girl and waited on her and sent her gifts. She was flattered by his attention but her heart was promised to another man—a cheerful shoemaker whose little shop was but two streets from her home.

The next day, the bodies of the shoemaker and the girl were found, stabbed and broken, at the bottom of a well…

If you add in the fact that I, too, was born on the first day of the Year of the Fire Tiger, you can see why that story got my attention.

When I called the owner of the website, she said she had some special news she wanted me to hear in person, so off I went to St. Louis. When I got there, the fortune-teller's address turned out to be Busch Stadium, home of the St. Louis Cardinals. So there I stood in the parking lot, feeling like a moron, while people streamed by me to see the Cardinals play the Chicago Bulls. Since the next bus back to San Francisco

Or was it the Blackhawks?

4.

wasn't going to leave for a couple of hours, I bought a cheap ticket and hiked up to the nosebleed section in left field.

There was a fat black lady with gold hoop earrings and polyester pants sitting in the seat next to mine and chugging beer from a plastic cup. "So, Cathy Vickers shows up at last." She belched and I realized she was wearing a luckyfortuneforyou.com t-shirt. "You can call me Auntie Joe, Sugar. I've been expecting you."

Imagine somebody completely astonished. Now imagine hitting them in the face with a dead catfish. Now imagine their expression. That's what was on my face. "But, but . . . I only bought my ticket five minutes ago," I said weakly. "How did you know I would show up here?"

"What about the words 'fortune-teller' is hard for you to understand?" Auntie Joe said. "Come on, Blue! Are you blind?" she shouted at the umpire, moments before the pitcher threw the ball. A second later the umpire called a strike and the fans around us groaned. "That's why I needed you to come out here in person. You needed to understand that when I say I can see the future, child, I ain't just whistling Dixie."

My brain was cramping like it was in labor and the baby was stuck. "I was expecting you to be Chinese," I whimpered.

"Oh, I'm every kind of psychic that pays, honey," Auntie Joe said indulgently. "I got businesses to cater to every kind of clientele. Chinese I Ching, voodoo dolls, Gypsy tarot card reading, you name it. I even got a nice little application my software dude programmed that can tell your fortune from the spam in your junk mail folder," she said. "Anyway—about Mr. Tsao. If he can't marry you, he *will* kill you. You know that, don't you?"

5.

The look on her face said she wasn't kidding. I gulped. It wasn't the romantic marriage proposal of every girl's dreams, that's for sure. On the plus side, Tsao had become an immortal when he was still a young man, so it didn't feel like being hit on by a dirty old guy. He was handsome, sophisticated, and very, very rich. On the down side, he was apparently a psychopathic killer, and, just to make things especially weird, he was Victor's dad. That's right: the man stalking me was my boyfriend's father.

Ew.

As you can imagine, the whole encounter with Auntie Joe had me pretty shaken up, even before she dropped the bomb about my father.

But I don't want to think about that part yet.

Recap over.

Just Past Midnight (Hour of the Bus Zombies)

The point is, I had a lot to think over on my way home from St. Louis. Me and a glum handful of other losers shuffled onto the bus and showed our tickets to the driver. There weren't many people getting on this particular bus, especially since it was delayed by six hours of mechanical breakdown, but on the bright side, at least I had a whole row to myself. Ah, back again into that familiar Greyhound smell: "dirty bathroom" was the foreground scent, of course, punching through an underlying aroma of cheap motel room, with an added fragrance of gasoline and topped off with a delicate hint of strangers' socks. I was contemplating a line of fashion accessories to go with the experience—perhaps

6.

mascara in "Tire-Skid Black" and eye shadow in "Dazzling Dashboard Blue."

I dropped into my seat and wriggled out of my backpack, which was currently stuffed to bulging, like one of those pictures of a snake that's eaten a goat or a filing cabinet or something. I had crammed the backpack full of enough clothes for five days, a mixed bag of art supplies (pencils, pastels, charcoal sticks, fixative, erasers, etc.), my purse, my sketchbook, and a printout of the pages of my diary that covered the whole strange Victor saga, from the moment he dumped me to the day I found out he was a) immortal, b) inexplicably still in love with me, and c) going to be trapped like a Mad Scientist in a dungeon lab for the foreseeable future.

I was trying to figure out what to do about Tsao in particular and immortals in general. I had printed out my diary thinking that on a two-day bus ride I could pore over those pages, as well as all the extra documents and clues I had found, filched, and stolen, and I would Discover Important New Facts by Paying Close Attention to Them. What really happened is that I stared out the bus window a lot and made killer doodles on the printouts. Careful analysis has never been my long suit.

The fact is, my whole life felt weirdly out of focus. I had a boyfriend I never saw. I missed him terribly—the touch of his hand, the way he laughed at my jokes, and the way he made me feel like I was always the most fascinating person in the room. But Victor was trapped working under the thumb of the most powerful immortal I knew, Ancestor Lu. Ancestor Lu wanted to bring eternal life to everyone, and was perfectly happy to murder anybody who got in the way of this benevolent plan. His motivational strategy for

7.

Victor was to tell him that if the research didn't go well, I would be killed.

This seemed to work on Victor, but it was a lot of guilt for one girl to carry. A bikini-wearing nun caught betting on dog fights would not feel the guilt I was carrying around at the idea that Victor was strapped to a table somewhere getting chunks of his liver scooped out on a regular basis on my account. Plus, if you're at home keeping score of my romantic troubles, don't forget the thing about Victor's dad being a psychopathic killer with a crush on me. I guess all relationships have their obstacles, but if you come whining to me with the old "my boyfriend is allergic to my cat" complaint, don't expect a lot of sympathy.

Just the plain existence of immortals left me unbalanced. On one hand, it was pretty neat to learn that the world was full of wonders and mysteries I had never imagined, but as a practical matter my life was more boring than it had ever been. I was out of high school and broke, with no sign of a good job coming. Worst of all, according to Auntie Joe, my father hadn't died of a heart attack two years ago, like the doctor had told me.

According to Auntie Joe, he had probably been murdered.

8.

Double Trouble

A blond girl about my own age was curled up in the seats across the aisle from me. Her gray sweatshirt said **Double Trouble,** and I could smell the stale cigarette smoke on it. She was wearing a pair of ratty blue jeans, grimy at the hems like she'd been wearing them for days. She used cheap blue eye shadow and lots of it. The last remains of a bruise were fading on her right cheek. I looked up and found she was watching me with pickpocket's eyes.

The calculating look instantly disappeared. "Hey there, my name's Jewel!" she said, giving me a big ol' smile. "Say, I don't suppose you might have fifty cents or something for a candy bar?"

"Uh—"

"I have to eat a little bit real regular on account of I have these issues with my blood sugar. My whole family's like that, we get diabetes unless we're real careful. Mamaw—she isn't really Mom's momma but we call her that—she lost a leg from it. Started to rot and they had to cut it off. Then she went blind," Jewel said. "So I need to eat if I can," she added.

My mother is a nurse. She says giving money to panhandlers is a waste of time. Whatever the con is, every dime of it gets spent on liquor and drugs. She sees kids like Jewel all the time. They get stoned or drunk and then they get hurt and come into the emergency room because they don't have any health care to cover doctor visits. Welcome to America, land without public health insurance. That's why they call it the home of the brave.

All the time Jewel was talking I was staring straight down. No eye contact at all.

10.

"I had me some spending money for the trip only I gave it to this guy who said he really needed it because he had to make this car payment which he could have done only he had loaned some money to a buddy. I forget the exact story."

Pause.

"Plus the ticket cost way more than it should have. I don't know if maybe the fare sign on the bus was messed up or something."

Pause.

I finally looked up at her. "I don't have any money."

Big double take.

"Oh! I'm sorry! You and me, we're in the same boat, then!" Jewel's voice was friendly, but her eyes were hard. "That's funny, ain't it? Here I am, telling you my story, only you could just be telling me yours, couldn't you? On account of you got nothing in that purse of yours but…hair ties and lipsticks." I was back to staring down at my sketchbook, but I could feel her cold little eyes pricing out the leather jacket Victor had given me and the silk shirt I had found at a thrift store. "Not a dime to spare, neither one of us," she said. "What are the odds?"

butt
out !

San Francisco Venture Capital Symphony— Emma Cheung, Guest Conductor

Mercifully, my cell phone rang at that moment. I fished it out of my purse and checked the caller ID. It was Emma.

"Cathy!" she shouted, over a roar of crowd noise. "My phone says you tried to call nine times!"

"Seven, tops."

"We were at the symphony!" Traffic noises mingled with crowd sounds; she must have been calling from the sidewalk right outside the symphony doors. "How's your conference going?"

"Conference?" I groped around the cobwebby attic of my brain, trying to remember my cover story. Basically, I had gone to St. Louis because I figured Tsao was a psychopath. It seemed untactful to say this, however, because besides being Victor's dad, Tsao was the only investor in Emma's company, DoubleTalk Wireless. He was also currently her only source of income and therefore her new best friend.

Awkward.

So I had given her the same lie I worked out for my mother. "The Business of Art conference!" I said, finally remembering my own BS. "Oh, it's been great. Monterey is so beautiful!"

"I thought you said the conference was in Santa Cruz."

"Yes, that's right," I babbled, as St. Louis slid by my darkened window. "We, uh, took a day trip. To the aquarium."

"You went to the Monterey Aquarium to discuss the business of art?"

"Yes. Whales," I said desperately. "There's a lot of money in whales these days. Endangered species generally. People want pictures of them before they go extinct, you know."

12.

Glancing across the aisle, I saw Miss Double Trouble smirking at me. I switched the phone to my other ear and turned my back on her. "I'm thinking of painting lemurs," I told Emma.

"Lemurs?"

"Ring-tailed ones," I said.

"Wow," Emma said. "Uh … great! So … why did you call exactly?"

"Is Tsao standing next to you?"

"No, he's still in the lobby talking with this VC we had dinner with. VC stands for venture capitalist." I could hear the smug little smile in her proper London accent.

"You're really enjoying this, aren't you?" I said. "The business meetings. Going to the symphony. Dinner with Individuals of High Net Worth."

She laughed. "Honestly, Cathy, when my dad showed up on my doorstep broke, my whole 401(k) flashed before my eyes."

"Listen, about Tsao—"

A car honked in the street behind Emma. "He takes me seriously, you know? I mean, I always thought I had interesting ideas. But nobody ever *noticed* before."

"I did!"

"It's so funny, the difference it makes just to be *seen*," Emma burbled. "It makes you feel more real. That's what Tsao does for me. Anyway, what were you going to say about him?"

"Uh … nothing," I lied. I cast around for a change of subject. "Listen, Emma, do you think it's possible that there are immortals who aren't Chinese?" Fat black ladies who drink beer, for instance …

"Oh, sure. The only genetic variations worth mentioning between different races of people are all found in Africa.

13.

14.

That was nature's lab, if you will, and even there all human genotypes can crossbreed. I would imagine the gene is spread pretty evenly throughout the world, wouldn't you?"

"That makes sense," I said, as if biology was one of those courses I had paid attention in. "Listen, do you remember that site we found, luckyfortuneforyou.com?"

"The funny one?"

"Yeah. Listen, I wrote her an email," I stammered. "And asked about my dad."

"Cathy! Good grief!" Emma scolded. "What's next? Tarot cards? You didn't spend *money*, did you?"

"No!" At least, not if you don't count round-trip bus fare and food for five days. "Of course not! The point is, she said something about my dad that got me thinking." I could still see plump Auntie Joe, looking sideways over her plastic cup of beer at me with eyes that seemed every day of a thousand years old. "She said, *Do you really think his death was an accident?*"

"Cathy, she's an entertainer," Emma said gently. "She's just trying to freak you out, thrill you. Set you up so you call her 1-900 number or pay for a live consultation."

"Maybe," I said, unconvinced. "But I can't stop thinking that maybe he didn't die of natural causes after all. Maybe he was murdered."

MY FATHER

Leaves flutter and whisper overhead, letting shifting coins of sunlight through. And I can hear the long hiss of the grass growing up from my father's grave.

Sisters Under the Skin

Tsao came out of the symphony lobby and Emma said she had to go. I flipped my cell phone closed and stuck it back in my purse. Most of the people on the bus seemed to have fallen asleep as we rocked and rattled our way through the long Missouri night.

"I heard you talking about your dad," Jewel said in the darkness.

"I beg your pardon?"

"My daddy's in prison. Some kind of fraud or something. He said he always meant to put the money back only this friend of his who was supposed to help him out couldn't make it on account of some accident. He's probably lying." Everyone around us was asleep and dreaming. The bus was dark except for the track lights on the floor; I could barely make out Jewel's dim profile across the aisle. Just the sound of her quiet voice drifting up like cigarette smoke in the darkness. "I knew as soon as I saw you we had something in common. People from broken families are kin, I always think…"

In the darkness, Jewel kept talking. She had a lot of stories and most of them seemed to start, "I knew this guy once…" According to Jewel, her mom had four kids by three different fathers. The mom had just gotten out of jail, again, and was turning her life around, again. She'd found Jesus again, too, but like all the men in her life, he seemed to be a bit unreliable.

"So maybe your daddy's in jail," Jewel said, "and your momma's living with Boyfriend Number Nine. And at least he's a nice drunk, not like some of the others, and the other kids at school … there's no point trying to explain it to them. I told this social worker once, they're so innocent you can't even talk to them. It's like there's a whole world that is invisible to them. You can like those kids and all, but you can't be close," she said. "But you and me, we're like sisters under the skin."

Hour of the All-Night Burger Joint

In middle of the night the bus crept into Springfield and eased into the station with a series of pings and a wheezing sigh like a fat man settling into a recliner. Straight out the front window was a sign for

open 24 hours

Bus Station Burgers

yum!

Home of the big wheel bun!

We both stared at it hungrily.

"Well, I guess I'll go see if I can find someone who can lend me a little money," Jewel said, to nobody in particular. "Just for an envelope and stamps to write my dad. I try to write almost every day. He says it means the world to him on account of most of the guys in jail, they're real jealous of my letters because their kids hardly come to visit or write them at all, he says."

I pulled my eyes away from the Bus Station Burgers sign. "I'm not going to give you any money," I said.

"I wasn't asking you, was I? Did you hear me ask?" she said belligerently. "I said I was going to borrow a couple of bucks inside for some stamps and an envelope. You might try listening a little harder to what other people are saying," she said.

The driver got off the bus and trudged into the station for some food. I waited until Jewel went to the bathroom and then snuck off the bus, quick as a cockroach, and scuttled into Bus Station Burgers. I got a Just Say Cheese! (Burger) and ate it there, threw out the wrapper and wiped my hands before I left the restaurant. I stealth-ninja'd my way over to the Ladies, so it would look like I was just coming back from the bathroom.

When I returned to my seat Jewel stared at me coldly, like she could smell Special Sauce on my breath. "Thought you said you didn't have any money," she said.

Ready, Aim ... *Draw!*

Sometimes, the only way to keep from getting run over is to go on the attack. I swore under my breath, dug out my sketchbook and pencils, fixed Jewel with my best gunslinger's stare and started to draw.

"What the hell are you doing?" Jewel said.

"Making you immortal," I growled, sketching her in with quick slashes of charcoal. For the first time since we'd met, she was the one who looked off balance.

In the Desert

Daybreak, somewhere in Oklahoma. I woke up with a mouthful of upholstery, a crick in my neck, and a left leg that had gone numb. Cautiously I sat up, feeling stiff and grimy,

17.

like a Bus Rider Barbie that had been lost under the bed for too long. On the seat next to me was my purse with my cell phone inside. Next to that, my backpack, with a few pages of my diary sticking out.

Waitasec.

I squinted a little harder. The diary pages were upside down. I tried to remember if I had left them like that before I fell asleep.

The blood was seeping back into my left leg, making for a jolly flush of pins and needles. I swore some and then checked my phone. One text message.

Hey kiddo—Mom here. Jst off shift, didn't want to call in cas u were asleep. Hope u r liking the biz-art course.

I hve anoter jb for u when u get back. Restaurnt. Maybe u cn make it 3 wks w/out getting fired.

A mother's confidence—what can beat that?

I wrote a quick return message and then stuffed the phone back in my purse and fumbled for my sketchbook.

No sketchbook.

That woke me up. I swore with more enthusiasm, sat bolt upright, and looked around. Across the aisle, Jewel was paging lazily through my drawings. She turned the book

18.

around and pointed to one of the sketches I had done in the middle of the night. "This is supposed to be me, isn't it?" I lunged for my book but she pulled it just out of range. "Now, now. Don't be grabby."

"Give that back!"

"What's the magic word?"

"Give that back or I'll have the bus driver throw you under the wheels," I snarled.

"That's better," Jewel said, handing over the sketchbook. "You're really good. You could sell some of these, I bet."

"Boy, you really think about money a lot, don't you?"

"My mother doesn't pay my rent," Jewel shot back. Ow! Touché. "Listen, I used to know this guy who published his own comic books and stuff like that. If you wanted to give me fifty bucks for expenses, I could put together a portfolio for you and see if he was interested in hiring you on." I gave her a look that was supposed to say, *"I will never be happy until I see you sprinkled with barbecue sauce and staked out on top of a fire ant mound."* "Twenty bucks," Jewel said. "If you don't need color photocopies."

"Thanks, but I'll take care of it."

She shrugged. "Your choice."

I still hadn't seen her eat.

19.

No Good Deed Goes Unpunished (Hour of the Egg McMuffins)

Amarillo, Texas. There was a McDonald's not far from the station. I bought two boxes of hash browns, two OJs and two Egg McMuffins and brought them back to the bus. I took out one set and put it on my seat, then handed the rest across the aisle in the McDonald's bag.

Jewel (hostile): "What's this?"

"Breakfast." Me still holding the bag.

"You think there's something wrong with me? Is that what you think?"

"I think you're hungry."

She slapped the bag onto the floor. "There's nothing wrong with me." Eyes hard. No Texas accent.

"You said—"

"Hey, if you don't want to give me a dime, that's your business. I don't want your damn food."

I ate both the Egg McMuffins right in front of her. Slowly.

*

"I figured you out," I said ten minutes later, balling up the McDonald's bag and licking my fingers. "It's all about the con, for you. As long as you're conning me, that's OK. You've got some self-respect." Outside the bus the desert stretched out flat under the Texas sun like a battered woman lying low. "But if I give you food—man, then you're just pathetic, aren't you?"

Jewel looked at me. "Shut up," she said. Accent gone again.

The Lioness (Hour of the Carbonated Kill)

That afternoon Jewel brought me a Dr Pepper. We were somewhere in New Mexico, and we were only in the station fifteen minutes, but somehow Jewel hopped back on the bus with a bulging bag of food from Taco Bell and two ice-cold Dr Peppers, one of which she tossed to me.

I checked her out. Her hair was slicked back like she'd wet it at a restroom tap. "Do I want to know how you came by this?"

<grinning> "Shut up and drink."

"How come I rate now?"

"Hey, I'm like a lioness. I make a kill, the whole herd shares the meat." The lioness ripped into her bag of Taco Bell like she was tearing the throat out of a gazelle. Halfway through a taco she looked up with trickles of grease running down her chin. "You too good to take a can of pop from me?"

"Not exactly." I held out the can she had tossed to me, and popped the lid. Dr Pepper sprayed in her face. She shrieked, liberally spattering the bus with taco meat, shredded lettuce, and genuine processed cheese product. Then she let out a string of swear words that would make a sailor blush. Then she started to laugh. Dr Pepper and taco juice dripped down her face. I laughed too.

The rest of the passengers on the bus turned around to stare at us like we were crazy. Seeing all those bored, annoyed faces made it impossible not to laugh more. The two of us, me and Jewel, wiping ourselves off with napkins from the Taco Bell and laughing so hard we could barely breathe.

21.

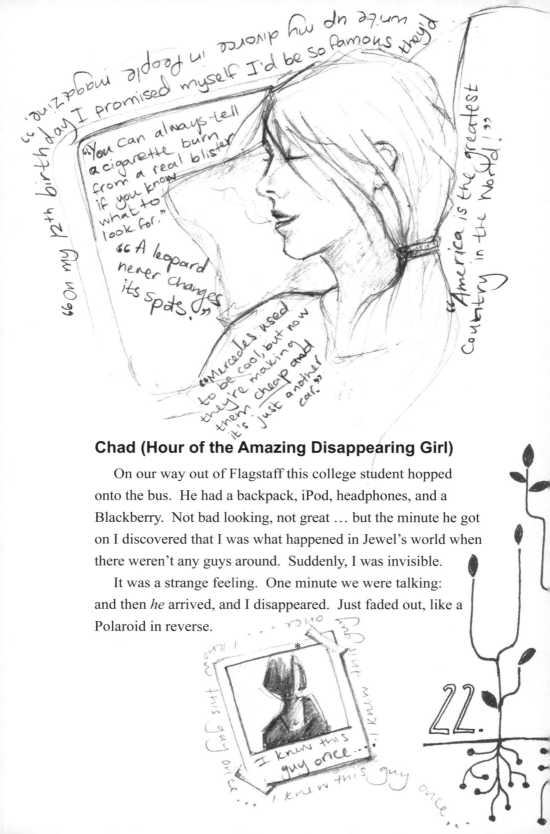

"On my 12th birthday I promised myself I'd be so famous they'd print my divorce in People magazine."

"You can always tell a cigarette burn from a real blister if you know what to look for."

"A leopard never changes its spots."

"Mercedes used to be cool, but now they're making them cheap and it's just another car."

"America is the greatest country in the World!"

Chad (Hour of the Amazing Disappearing Girl)

On our way out of Flagstaff this college student hopped onto the bus. He had a backpack, iPod, headphones, and a Blackberry. Not bad looking, not great … but the minute he got on I discovered that I was what happened in Jewel's world when there weren't any guys around. Suddenly, I was invisible.

It was a strange feeling. One minute we were talking: and then *he* arrived, and I disappeared. Just faded out, like a Polaroid in reverse.

*

I knew this guy once … I knew this guy once … I knew this guy once … I knew this guy once …

22.

"His name's Chad. He's a business student at Arizona State. He's dumb, but kinda sweet." Jewel had moved up to Chad's row for the last few hours, but she stopped in the aisle to talk to me on her way back from the toilet. She stood swaying with the rock of the bus, her hips moving in her tight jeans, dirty blond hair, dirty fingers, grinning. A lioness hunting. "God, I wish I had some mouthwash."

I watched her walk up to Chad's row. She pulled out a pillow and a blanket from the overhead compartment. Then she nestled down beside him and spread the blanket over their laps.

Graduation Present

When I woke up next, it was morning. It was painfully bright, as if someone was pushing little thumbtacks of sunshine into my eyes. Jewel was sitting across the aisle from me again. No sign of Chad. He must have gotten off the bus.

Jewel smiled, all friendly-like again. I felt my hackles rise. "Hey, Cathy?" she said. "I'm having a little trouble with my … with this." Jewel stuck a Blackberry phone into my face. "It says it will play games, but I can't quite figure out how to…" I narrowed my eyes at her. "It ought to be on a Games menu or sumthin'," she said, her voice as Texas as biscuits and gravy.

"This looks like the phone your date was carrying last night," I said. "Chad."

"It was a present from my dad," Jewel said. "Graduation present."

"The dad you said was in jail?"

"He bought it for me online."

"I thought you said you dropped out."

"I did. I went back and challenged the exams. I knew this guy that did it, so I studied up. I didn't pass with flying colors, you know. But I passed."

I looked at her. "Un-hunh."

"We had a graduation party, it was great. I think my folks were scared to death I wasn't ever going to amount to anything, but then when I passed my tests the whole family came over and we all went down to Tony Roma's for barbecue and we *laughed*…"

"They must have been very proud," I said dryly.

"Relieved is more like it."

Jewel put the Blackberry away and didn't ask me for help again.

I wondered if her dad was really in jail, or if he was dead like mine.

Beauty Is Only Skin Deep… (Hour of the Nevada State Patrol)

Another bus station. I woke from a dull drowse to find Jewel sitting next to me and reading more pages from my diary. "Hey!" I said, struggling upright. "You can't—"

"Uh oh," she said, pointing out the window. "Cops."

Two Nevada state troopers in black boots and sunglasses stepped onto the bus. A hard electric crackle ran down my spine. The last time two cops came to talk to me they had been working for Ancestor Lu. They kidnapped me, drove me out into the countryside where nobody would ever know what happened to me, and turned me over to be shot. Somehow the sight of those dark blue uniforms wasn't too reassuring for me anymore.

Chill out, I told myself. Chad must have figured out who

CRIME SCENE DO NOT ENTER CRIME SCENE

"Told you I didn't take nothin'"!

stole his Blackberry, that's all. Now Jewel was going to go to jail, over some stupid business-school geek's two-hundred-dollar phone. Part of me was relieved. I'm not proud of that, but it's true.

After a brief conversation with the bus driver, the cops walked back to our row. Jewel looked up, guilty as sin. "What do you want? I ain't done nuthin'." They asked to look in her bags. "I ain't got nuthin'! Hey—you can't just look in my stuff! You need a warrant to look in there!"

The cops ignored her. They grabbed her backpack and started searching through it, pulling out an address book, a pair of shorts and a T-shirt, a hairbrush and some tampons, a pocketknife and a bra. All this time Jewel was shifting back and forth in her seat, not making eye contact, saying how she hadn't done nuthin'.

That Texas accent laid on with a trowel.

POLICE ONLY   DO NOT CROSS POLICE

… and after all that, they didn't find a damn thing.

The cops left the bus, shaking their heads. The Greyhound rumbled out of the station and we were on the road again. Jewel looked like the cat who ate the canary. She hadn't stopped grinning since the police disappeared in a cloud of diesel exhaust behind us.

I broke down. "Where is it?"

Lazy grin. "Where's what?"

"The Blackberry. Look, I promise I won't tell anyone. I just want to know what you did with it. Were they close?"

"Cops?" She laughed. The southern accent had disappeared again. "A cop couldn't find his ass with both hands."

25.

"You looked pretty worried."

"It's the *cops,* dummy. Innocent people always look guilty when they're talking to cops." Jewel gave me a pitying look and tapped one dirty finger on my forehead. "Beauty is only skin deep," she drawled, putting her Texas accent back on like a fake fingernail, "but dumb goes clean through to the bone."

Forever

"Hey," I said a while later.

Jewel looked up at me. She was reading a shiny new copy of *People* magazine that she had probably shoplifted from the bus station store in Las Vegas. "Yeah?"

"What would you do if you could live forever?"

She thought it over. "Kill myself?" The whine of the bus motor crept up another note as the Greyhound strained to climb up into the Sierras. "I don't know," Jewel said at last. "Forever just seems like a long time to be on the road."

Missing in Action

I woke up in the middle of the night. I had no idea where we were. Maybe California. Maybe hell. I staggered to the bathroom and splashed some water on my face to wake up.

"I don't think your daddy was murdered," Jewel said as I came back to my seat. She had the hood on her sweatshirt pulled up, and her face was a darker shadow within. I realized she had my backpack next to her and my diary pages spread out over the seat.

26.

"What did you say?"

"Your dad. You were telling your friend maybe he was killed, but I think he probably just skipped out on you."

"Give me that stuff back!" I said, grabbing at my printouts.

Jewel passed me a copy of Victor's forged birth certificate, the one I had taken from his house earlier in the spring. Then she held up a copy of my father's death certificate. "The same doctor signed both of these."

I grabbed the death certificate. "Don't you ever touch my stuff again."

"It's a con, Cathy. If the birth certificate smells, the death certificate's gotta stink a little too, yeah?" I froze. Jewel kept talking. "How did you say you found your dad? Dead of a heart attack in his studio, right?"

Memories like a handful of dropped photographs: my father lying on the hardwood floor, blue lips in a gray face. The doctor crouching over him with a professional frown, *'heart attack dear, there's nothing you could have done.'* Milk from my broken glass spattered all over, white drops on the hardwood floor.

"And then a doctor friend showed up and called the ambulance, right?" Jewel said. "The way I figure it, your dad waits until you come into the room. He holds his breath, there's a bit of makeup to make him look like crap, you know. The doctor is in on the scam—as soon as he hears you scream he just 'happens' to drop by."

"Shut up," I said.

"You're in shock, the doctor pushes by you. He says, 'Oh my god he's dead!' and shoves you out of the room. Is that how it happened?"

"Shut up." But that was exactly how it had happened. I had found my dad dead. My mom was out of town. The doctor said he heard me scream. He said he was a friend of my father's, too, but I had never seen him before in my life.

Jewel shrugged. "Middle-aged suburban dad decides he wants to hump a younger model and splits," she said. "It happens all the time."

I was so angry I could barely breathe. "My dad would never leave me."

"Mine did."

"But—" I bit my tongue.

"But you're *different*," Jewel drawled. "Your daddy *loved* you."

"Don't … just don't talk to me," I said.

"Are you *crying*?" Jewel said. "You think anyone gives a shit? I'm just telling you the score, Cathy. It's what friends do." Jewel turned away. "Go ahead and cry then. Feel sorry for yourself. Ain't nobody else gonna do it for you," she said. "Anybody who tells you different is selling something."

"I hate you," I said.

"What's funny to me is, you were all excited when you thought your daddy might have been murdered. I tell you maybe he's alive, and *now* you cry. Because your feelings are hurt," she said. "Swear to God, you'd be happier if he was dead."

I jumped out of my seat and lunged for her. Quick as a snake she grabbed my hand and bent my wrist around, hard. I dropped to my knees. With her other hand Jewel grabbed me by the hair and jerked my face up to look into hers. "Get back to your seat." Her voice was full of contempt. "Decent folks are trying to sleep."

28.

Dawn

Hours passed.

I got out Victor's fake birth certificate, the one that claimed he'd been born in 1980. It was signed by a Dr. David Parkinson. Then I got out my dad's death certificate. David Parkinson.

It could be a coincidence. It was a very common name. I stared at the two signatures. They were the same. Obviously, unmistakably the same.

Maybe Jewel was right, but I just couldn't understand *why*. Say my dad had a midlife crisis. There were divorce courts to handle that stuff. And even if he was tired of Mom, wouldn't he at least want to see me on weekends?

God, Cathy. Listen to yourself.

"Hey," Jewel murmured, some time around four in the morning. I scrambled upright and brought up my fists, but she stayed in her seat on the other side of the aisle. "Sugar, I am so sorry," Jewel said softly. "I had no call to go be mean to you. I got to thinking about some things and I let my temper get the best of me." Her head was bent and her voice was humble. I turned the reading light toward her face. Incredibly, there was actually a tear on her cheek. "You're the only person that's been halfway nice to me in a long time," she said. "I'm sure your daddy died just like you thought."

Goddamn it, I was crying again. "What do you even want from me?"

"You're so smart, and talented. And nice," Jewel said. "I wish I could be like you."

The Lady Vanishes (Hour of the Missing Book)

The next time I woke up, we were in the bus station in San Jose and Jewel was gone. The Greyhound blanket she had curled up in for two days had disappeared. There was no sign of her backpack, no cardboard pizza box or Dr Pepper can under the seat.

I made the bus driver wait while I ran into the station, but there was no trace of her there, either. It was as if she had never existed. I was just psyching myself up to look for her in the men's washroom when a voice came over the PA system telling me my bus would leave without me if I wasn't back in sixty seconds. I got back on board and sank into my seat, weirdly upset that Jewel had disappeared without even saying good-bye.

My eye fell on my backpack. Suddenly suspicious, I hefted it. It was unnaturally light. "Goddamn it," I said.

My diary was gone, and my cell phone, too.

I found the stolen Blackberry at the bottom of my backpack. I had a vivid flashback to Jewel smirking at me when I asked her where she had hidden it. Now I had my answer: it had been there in my backpack all along. If the cops had thought to search my stuff, I might still be sitting in a Nevada jail. "Goddamn it," I said again.

I guess in her mind, giving me the Blackberry evened up her stealing my phone. Or maybe she was already calling the cops with a tip and they would be waiting for me in Burlingame with a warrant. I looked at the Blackberry to see if Jewel had made any calls or sent any messages after Chad had left the bus. Bingo. She had sent one email to **dietrying83@gmail.com**. At least I had one place to start if I wanted to track her down.

Sisters under the skin, she had called us. And now she was out in the world somewhere, with my cell phone and all my secrets, and I had lost my book.

32.

Blackberries

I picked up the Blackberry again. It felt weird to be using someone else's phone, but I needed help and I needed it now. I punched in Emma's number.

"Hullo?" she said, in her puzzled British voice. "Who is this?"

"Hey, it's Cathy."

"Caller ID says you've changed your name to Chad," Emma observed. "It must have been an exciting week."

"Yeah, somebody stole my phone and I'm calling on a Blackberry I, uh, borrowed."

"A Blackberry? *You?* What's the model number?"

I told her.

"Oh—that's like nine months old," she said, disappointed. In Emma's world, electronic gadgets have the shelf life of unrefrigerated yogurt.

"Listen, I'm going to be at the bus station in about twenty minutes. Could you pick me up?" After she said yes, I took a deep breath and plunged into my real business. "There's something else. I was looking at my dad's death certificate, and Victor's faked birth certificate, and the same doctor is on both. David Parkinson."

33.

There was a brief pause as Emma digested this information. "That's a bit of a coincidence."

"Yeah, that's what I thought. Would you do your internet stalker thing on him and see what you turn up?"

"Absolutely," Emma murmured. Her fingers were already tapping away on her computer keyboard by the time I hung up.

OK, I had a ride back from the station and the investigation into the mysterious Dr. Parkinson was underway. Jewel had taken the printout of my diary from this past spring, which was no big deal because I still had that saved on my hard drive. What I couldn't replace were the doodles I had put all over the printout in my endless bus ride, and, much more importantly, the stuff I had filched from Victor—the old photos and letters. Emma had scanned all the stuff in and had it archived on the private side of www.DoubleTalkWireless.com. But I felt awful for having lost so many things that were precious to Victor, like the letters from his sister, Frances. Worst of all was having lost my father's death certificate, which I had carried around with me since he passed away.

I really, really wanted to hunt Jewel down and do things to her with a staple gun until she begged for mercy and gave me my damn stuff back.

ArtGirl Detective Strikes Again! (Hour of the Little White Lie)

First step: looking at that email address Jewel had sent to before she disappeared. The instant I picked up the Blackberry, it buzzed indignantly like an Anti-Peeper Alarm that had caught me red-handed. I dropped it with a little squeak. It landed

face down on the seat beside me and buzzed again like a bee
trapped under a pillow *Mph-bzz! Bzzmzph!*

I only dared to pick it up when I was quite sure it had
stopped vibrating. A new message was showing on the screen.

```
J! u
promised 2 call. mom is
freaking out. Where r u?
denny
```

J for Jewel, obviously. The guy she had messaged was
texting her back. His name was Denny and he was her brother,
probably, to judge by the message.

At this point I should make it clear that even though Jewel
had screwed me over and taken all my stuff, I had absolutely
no business picking up that Blackberry, or typing a message.
That would be Wrong …

… although you could make the argument that learning
a little more about Jewel was a legitimate part of getting my
phone and diary back, couldn't you?

I hit Reply and thumbed in:

I'm in San Jose.

And then—I don't know why—I added,

UR lying about mom.
J

The Blackberry buzzed again in less than a minute.

```
She wud b freaking out if
she was sober. I said u were
```

```
staying w/ friends.  Can u
get home?
```

This time it was easy to know what Jewel would say.

I can take care of myself.

I wondered if the brother was younger than Jewel, or older.
I guessed older. The Blackberry buzzed again. I was about to
read the next message when I abruptly remembered that what I
was doing here was fairly creepy. Cathy Vickers, Voyeur Girl.
What would I be up to next? Drilling peepholes into the boys'
locker room? This had definitely gone too far. I imagined
poor Denny on the other end of the line, the responsible older
brother who had taken on the burden of holding the family
together. At the very least, I should tell the poor guy he hadn't
actually been talking to his sister. I picked up the Blackberry
and read:

```
"take care of myself" = no $ to
get home, right?  Stick tight +
give me ur address.  Ill come
get u as soon as I make bail.
```

 'gulp

Bail! Denny!

```
No big deal.  Just a fight.
```

I could totally see Jewel
rolling her eyes, exasperated.

Again?

```
I was coming out of a bar n
this guy was beating up his
gf.  Told him to stop.  He
didn't. We danced. No bg dl.
```

36.

I sat there, looking at the Blackberry. Why on earth would the cops pursue a case against Denny when he had just been trying to help a defenseless woman?

The girlfriend lied, you idiot. This thought popped into my head in Jewel's voice, as if she was standing there next to me. *When the cops showed up, the little slut took her boyfriend's side.*

But … why?

Because she's on the street. Because she's broke. Because she needs him, who knows. That's what trash like that does, Jewel's voice said. *Because if she rats the son of a bitch out to the police, he'll beat her up worse, or his friends will. Because she's a coward. Because that's what we do.*

Oh, Jewel.

Introducing Pete (Hour of Emma's New Guy)

Twenty minutes later I finally crawled off the Greyhound at the Burlingame station and staggered out into the California sunshine. Emma was waiting for me. Or, to be more precise, Emma and a boy.

This was a big deal.

Back in the eighth grade Emma had tried pining after a cute guy in her math class. One day he came over to her desk (passing Jenny Who Had Real Boobs Already) and asked her out for pizza. We were pretty excited about it—Emma even let me make her up to look cool and sophisticated, which I did by using enough eyeliner and hair mousse to outfit an emo band. Sadly, it turned out over a small pepperoni pizza that the boy was only interested in one thing: Emma's calculator. His wealthy parents had said he could have a motorbike if he made a B in math. For a moment Emma imagined being his tutor, spending quiet moments together whispering formulas in the privacy of his room, but it turned out he just wanted to pay her to *do* his homework.

Emma, of course, was Not That Kind of Girl. Having a boy peek at her homework was functionally the same as having a fat truck driver named Chuck look down her blouse. "I felt so *cheap*," she spluttered. "So … *violated*."

So to see her at the Greyhound station with a guy … *that* was interesting. "Welcome back," Emma said. "Pete's giving us a lift."

"Hey," Pete said. He was all elbows and knees and nervous energy. His eyes hadn't decided if they were going to be green or grey; his hair was sandy blond and disheveled, as if it had been claimed by the Nature Conservancy and declared off-limits to combs. I wondered where he fit in the grand scheme of things. Boyfriend? Study partner?

"Did you get any sleep? Are you tired? We're parked just outside," Emma said over her shoulder. "Pete's doing some programming for DoubleTalk."

Ah, I thought: *minion!* My world made sense again.

The three of us piled into Pete's monster-sized pickup truck. Check that—monster-sized *hybrid* pickup truck. Welcome to Northern California, home of the blue-collar vegan with a brewski in one hand and a tofu dog in the other. Obviously Emma and I couldn't talk about my immortal boyfriend or possibly murdered dad in front of this guy, but it was hard to think of another topic.

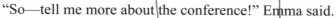

"So—tell me more about the conference!" Emma said.

"Conference?"

"The Business of Art, dummy. You *must* be tired." Oh, right, that. Sometimes keeping up with my own BS seems like a full-time job. I cringed inside, but Emma was all enthusiasm. "You know, your mom and I were talking about this seminar. She was so proud of you for really trying to do something practical with your art."

You know how when you flip over a rock, you find these horrible creepy-looking bugs underneath? I felt like whatever it is those bugs despise.

I took a deep breath. "Emma," I said.

"So, what was the most important thing you learned at the conference?"

So help me God, I meant to confess. But somehow the words, "Electronic storefronts!" came out of my mouth instead. "Your regular brick-and-mortar retail outlet has so little reach," I added.

"That's exactly what I always say!" No surprise there, as I was making up this spiel from half-remembered fragments of many impassioned Emma lectures.

"Brick-and-mortar retail outlet?" Pete said, puzzled. "Emma said you were a painter."

"Galleries, in my business," I said quickly. "Gallery owners charge a huge commission—fifty percent or more, sometimes. Plus if I hang pieces in a gallery, only people who physically come into the store will ever see them. But if I were to sell stuff on my own website, first of all I wouldn't have to pay a commission, and secondly people from all over the world

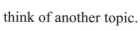

would be able to visit with just the click of a mouse!" I said this enthusiastically, as if I actually had a clue.

"The problem, obviously, is getting eyeballs on the site," Emma said. "Did they have any suggestions?"

"Well, uh … we got bogged down in website design and graphic appeal. You can imagine, with a conference room full of graphic designers…" Emma rolled her eyes. "Still, I have a few ideas. The first thing I need is a name. A really great URL can make the difference between a smash hit and just another also-ran," I said knowledgeably.

"Cathy's Creations?" Emma suggested.

"Sounds like I sell bath soap."

"Good point. Um … 'Art's Desire'? Or 'Art to Art.' It's a pun," she explained.

"Open Art Surgery," Pete suggested.

"You're such a boy," Emma said.

"Art Attack!"

"Do you need help building the site?" Emma said. "I could loan you Pete."

"Er—that's okay," I said quickly. "Mom lined up another regular job for me and I need the cash, so I'll be concentrating on that for the next couple of weeks."

"Liquidity versus capital," Emma said, shaking her head. "The ancient struggle."

Like I said, I had already burned through three jobs in the weeks since school had ended:

- The bakery job, where I got fired for not being able to make it in at 4 a.m. each morning. (*I'm not late,* as my dad used to say, *I'm just slightly displaced in time.*)
- The telephone solicitor job, where I got canned on my

first day for saying, "So basically you just *hate burn victims?"*

- The Burger Barn job, where I got fired for swearing. Over the loudspeakers. But honestly, that wasn't entirely my fault …

Flashback-ack-ack (Hour of the Escaped Boyfriend)

"Welcome to Burger Barn, how may I help you?"

I'd said that part on autopilot, staring down at my register. I was trying to break my personal record for Most Consecutive Customers Without Screwing Up. After three days on the job, the record was still about four, so intense concentration was called for.

I felt a finger touch me under the chin and tilt my face up. Victor was standing in front of my register at Burger Barn. "This job is a complete waste of your talents," he said, grinning, "but you sure look cute in overalls."

"Victor!?! But!?" I shook my head and tried to de-spazz. "Did you get a day off or something?"

"I snuck out. Ancestor Lu is on the other side of the world trying to recruit more people to The Project."

"Snuck out! If you get caught he'll…" I wasn't sure exactly what one immortal could do to another, but I was pretty confident Lu could make Victor hurt. "Why take the risk?"

"Ancestor Lu is very happy with me just now. Besides, I wanted to see you," Victor said simply. He brushed my cheek with the side of his hand and I felt myself start to flush.

"Hey, Mister," said the next person in line, a middle-aged

41.

woman with frown lines that made her look like a large mouth bass in a bad mood. "Hurry up and order already."

Victor ignored her. "I've been here for more than an hour just watching you work." He twisted a stray lock of my hair that had escaped from underneath my Burger Barn ball cap.

"You want some fries, you can stand in line," Grumpy Lady said. "You want anything else, get a motel."

I could feel myself blushing. "I should take your order."

"I'll have a Double Patty Doozie and a medium drink," Victor said, still smiling.

My stupid hands were shaking as I punched in the order. "How long can you be out of the lab before Lu notices? I get off my shift in two hours. Maybe we…"

Victor shook his head. "No, I have to get back. Although God knows, if I could do what I wanted…"

His hand felt hot on my skin. I passed his burger out to him. I could feel myself flushing as if it was me who had been lying under the heat lamp instead of the Double Patty Doozie. There were so many things I needed to say and I couldn't seem to find the words for any of them. "Victor? When are we going to—"

Victor cut me off. "Forever," he said, and his voice promised everything.

Fish Mouth coughed warningly and waved, trying to catch the eye of my manager.

I adopted what the Burger Barn employee training manual called *"your hearty 'Howdy!' voice"* and said, "Would you like anything else today, sir?"

"Just one more thing." Victor slid his hand behind my neck, pulled me forward over the top of the register and kissed me. On a scale of 1 to 10, that kiss was a 93. He kissed like

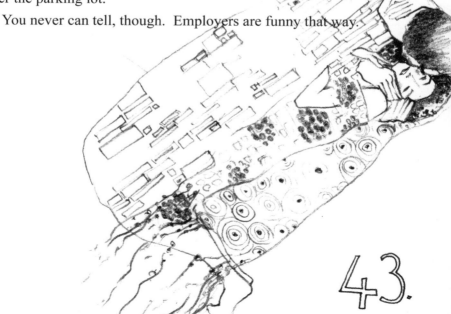

a man just out of prison; he kissed me like he'd been thinking of nothing but that kiss every lonely night for the five months since I had seen him last. That kiss lit me up for a timeless time, until Victor finally let his hand slide down my back and stepped away and I was left hanging breathlessly over the cash register with my eyes closed and my lips reaching out for his.

Someone whistled. Someone else cheered. Three guys I knew from school started clapping enthusiastically and the place went wild. I opened my eyes. Victor was walking out the door, grinning, and approximately eight thousand people were staring at me, all of them laughing and clapping except for one. "Oh, so THAT'S how you get a free burger," Fish Mouth sneered, at which point I realized Victor had walked off without paying. He knew it, too, the dog. I could see him waving at me through the glass doors.

With the benefit of hindsight, I realize that shouting, "Get your !#@*$^ butt back here and pay for your !#@*$^ burger!" was a mistake, but I still think I might not have been fired if I hadn't yelled it into the intercom system and broadcast it all over the parking lot.

You never can tell, though. Employers are funny that way.

43.

End Flashback (We Now Return You to Emma, Pete, and the Mysterious Doctor Parkinson…)

It was after the Burger Barn debacle that I decided to spend my few saved pennies and head to St. Louis. Now I was back home getting a ride in Pete's truck, as broke as the day I finished school and with no obvious way to get Victor out of Ancestor Lu's clutches and back into my life. I stared bleakly down the barrel of my so-called career. "One of the doctors at my mom's hospital is an investor in a restaurant downtown called *Fondue!*" I told Emma and Pete unenthusiastically. "I'm going to be a waitress. Mom says waitressing is a very transportable skill."

"I dunno," Emma said dubiously. "When it comes to you and the working world, I think the words 'customer service' should be a warning sign."

"Easy for you to say. You're going to the Berkeley School of Business to explore High Finance and International Relations," I said. "I'm going to get scalded with boiling cheese."

"I like cheese," Pete said.

Awkward silence.

We turned on to my street and came to a stop outside my house. Mom's Mercury was in the driveway—she would still be asleep inside. My mother worked the graveyard shift, so her alarm was usually set for four in the afternoon.

"Hey Pete," Emma said, piling out of the truck after me, "could you just wait for a minute while I talk to Cathy about something private?"

"Okeydoke." Pete gave a thumbs-up and reached for his radio.

"Do you actually pay him?" I asked as we walked up to the porch.

44

"Stock options," she said briskly. "Better than cash. Anyway, about your mysterious Dr. Parkinson. Turns out he is a plastic surgeon."

"Why the heck would a plastic surgeon be signing birth and death certificates?"

"Yeah, I wondered that, too," Emma said. "Anyway, Parkinson's been divorced twice. Filed for bankruptcy twice. Brought up on charges of insurance fraud once." She hesitated. "The business with your dad's death certificate is a little freaky, Cathy. Like, what are the odds Parkinson should be a shady character, *and* know Victor, *and*…"

"Just happen to walk into our house at the exact moment I found my dad's body," I finished.

"Did you ever see the body?" Emma asked delicately. "Afterward I mean?"

I shook my head. "He was cremated. The doctor said he would take care of it. By the time my mom got back from Mexico, we just had this urn." Emma looked at me. I knew what she was thinking: one set of ashes looks pretty much like any other. How convenient, Jewel would say. No body to identify.

"It would be interesting to know if Parkinson kept a file on your father," Emma said thoughtfully.

I watched Pete roll down the truck window and pretend not to be eavesdropping. "Yeah," I said, "I was just thinking the same thing."

Emma looked up at me, alarmed. "No," she said. "I recognize that tone of voice. Cathy, we are NOT breaking into this guy's office."

Pete stopped pretending not to be listening.

"Did I say anything about breaking in?" I said huffily.

45.

"We'll drop by during business hours. You distract him and I'll go through his files. Pete's eavesdropping on us, by the way. Pete, would you be willing to help make a distraction in a doctor's office?"

"Awesome," Pete said, leaning out of the window and grinning. "Emma told me you got these criminal impulses, but I figured it would take a while to show. Like being a werewolf or something."

"You stay out of this," Emma snapped. "Cathy!"

"You're right," I said. "I probably couldn't figure out the computerized records. *I'll* distract him—*you* go through the database. Pete, you could crack a bunch of medical files, couldn't you?"

"Cathy!" Emma shook a finger at me. "You're subverting a minor, or soliciting cybercrime, or something," she said firmly. "No, no, no. Absolutely not."

Pete drummed his fingers thoughtfully on the side of his truck. "I know a guy who cut some code for a medical clinic. I could do a little prep work, yeah."

Emma glared at him. "Don't encourage her! Listen, Cathy, there will be a receptionist, okay? And maybe a nurse or a file clerk or a medical technician."

"If there are lots of people, then it will just have to be a really good distraction," I said brightly. Emma stared at me, speechless. "Lunch tomorrow is my first shift at Fondue!" I said. "Why don't we meet up after that? You guys can pick me up at the restaurant."

"Great," Emma said gloomily. "I'll look up some good bail bondsmen tonight."

That's what I like about that girl. Always covering the practical angles.

47.

Home Again

I let myself through the front door, tiptoed through the house so I wouldn't wake up my mom, and crashed onto my bed, feeling how wonderful it was going to be to sleep somewhere that wasn't the seat of a Greyhound.

After a few minutes I checked my computer for messages, combing through five days of spam to see if there was anything new from Victor. No such luck. Well, of course, if I wanted a message from Victor, there were things I could do to encourage that ...

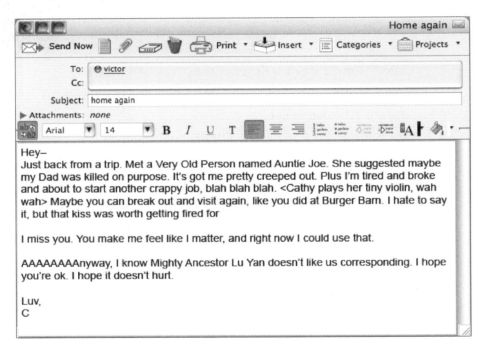

Hey—
Just back from a trip. Met a Very Old Person named Auntie Joe. She suggested maybe my Dad was killed on purpose. It's got me pretty creeped out. Plus I'm tired and broke and about to start another crappy job, blah blah blah. <Cathy plays her tiny violin, wah wah> Maybe you can break out and visit again, like you did at Burger Barn. I hate to say it, but that kiss was worth getting fired for

I miss you. You make me feel like I matter, and right now I could use that.

AAAAAAAAnyway, I know Mighty Ancestor Lu Yan doesn't like us corresponding. I hope you're ok. I hope it doesn't hurt.

Luv,
C

My mouse hovered over the Send button. It was a whiny letter—basically a naked attempt to force Victor to write back and say that living without me was like doing somersaults on a barbed wire trampoline. It was needy, desperate for

cheap medications are here...
ABSOLUTELY FREE!

reassurance, and not a little paranoid.

All in all, a very accurate portrait. Not flattering, perhaps. But accurate. I hit Send.

Then I got up from in front of my computer, threw my backpack on my bed, and staggered off to the shower.

Forty-five minutes later I was back, feeling much more like a human being and much less like something dragged out of the lost and found bin at the Greyhound station. My skin was damp and shiny and clean again. The bits of sweat-saturated compressed sock fuzz had all been washed away from between my toes, and my hair smelled pleasantly of honey, glycol, apricots, and Red Dye #5. Mm-hmm.

I moseyed over to the computer, still wearing a towel, and sat down expectantly to read Victor's anxious, tender, reassuring reply.

No email from Victor. Nothing. Nada. Zippo. Zilch.

There WAS a friendly letter offering to Enlarge my Man Parts. Not quite what I was looking for. I checked my junk mail filter. In the time I'd been away from my desk I had won five hundred dollars to spend in an online casino, been offered an impressive range of Canadian pharmaceutical products, and been selected to receive a bachelors degree from a Prestigious Unaccredited University ABSOLUTELY FREE. I lingered over that last spam. Honestly, the odds of getting a college diploma the old-fashioned way seemed depressingly remote.

Back to check my Inbox. Still empty.

Victor, answer me, you jerk.

It immediately occurred to me that he might not be at his desk looking at his computer. He might be strapped to a table while Ancestor Lu's medical techs were siphoning off his

This might be what you want...

Are you insecure?

Doctor Approved and Recommended!!!!

ENLARGE MY MAN PARTS

LADIES WILL LOVE YOU

JOIN THE MILLIONS

49.

blood, or sectioning his liver, or cutting out his pituitary glands. *Jesus, Cathy. Get it together.*

I shut down my email program. Victor would write back as soon as he could. Meanwhile, I had my own life to take care of. Tomorrow morning was my first shift at Fondue! Afterward, it would be time to check out the mysterious Dr. Parkinson and find out if Auntie Joe had been right when she said my father's death had been more than just a tragic accident.

I flipped on the TV. Pictures from our military overseas. A car bomb in a crowded marketplace, civilian casualties, two soldiers kidnapped while on patrol. Grim.

I meant to turn off the TV, but I fell asleep before I could find the remote.

The Adventures of FondueGirl! (Hour of the Artificial Enhancements)

Late the next afternoon Pete's truck was idling in front of the restaurant when I got off my shift. I pulled the door open and jumped inside.

"Oh, my god!" Emma said, staring at me aghast. "What are you wearing?"

"Traditional Swiss garb," I snarled. Actually, the uniforms at Fondue! would have passed for traditional Swiss clothing only if you went skiing in the Mission District of San Francisco. I had come into work wearing pants and a white shirt; now I had on a short, loose skirt, a frilly apron, and a peasant blouse cut to provide lots of scenery of the Alps, at least if you were built like Nora the Chain-Smoking Hostess.

In my case we weren't talking so much Alps as foothills. Or maybe prairie with the occasional gopher mound.

Emma's face was crinkling into a smirk. "And what have you got on your feet?"

"Clogs," I said belligerently. "Got a problem with that?"

"What happened to your real clothes?"

"A small kerosene fire and a lot of boiling cheese. Look, I don't really want to talk about it, okay? Let's just go to Dr. Parkinson's office and do this thing."

Pete was careful not to make eye contact, but he was grinning at the steering wheel pretty hard. "I vote she gets to do the distraction part."

"Shut up and drive," I said.

Twenty-five minutes later the nice lady trapped inside Pete's GPS navigation system announced that we had arrived at our destination. Pete picked a spot and parked.

"Wait a sec," Emma said. "We need a plan."

"Got it covered," I said. I reached into my purse, where I had a water balloon dyed red to make it look like blood on bursting, three sparklers I had purchased from the illegal fireworks place we saw on the way, a small tape recorder loaded with the sound of sirens, a wig, and a fully loaded lighter. "I'm ready," I said brightly.

"That's what I'm afraid of," Emma said. "What are you going to say to the receptionist?"

"I thought I'd just yell 'Fire!' and see what happened."

"Cathy!"

"You could say you were looking for a missing goat," Pete suggested, indicating my Swiss Miss outfit.

"Very funny," I griped. "Okay, so, you want a cover story.

51.

Like, why am I coming to see a plastic surgeon."

Emma looked at me over the tops of her little round glasses. I crossed my arms protectively in front of my chest. "No!"

"It *is* the obvious reason," Emma said, using her Reasonable Voice.

"There's nothing wrong with oranges," I said, quoting something my mother told me when I was fourteen.

"Mandarin oranges," Emma said. "Tell him you want grapefruits."

"I saw this thing on the internet about girls going in for butt enhancements," Pete volunteered unexpectedly.

Our heads swiveled to look at him.

"Apparently these girls want, you know, the round kind. They showed these panties with extra padding at the back, too."

"Where on the internet did you see this?" Emma said. Coldly.

He looked wounded. "I was just thinking about what you said the other day about Cathy's—"

"Let's just go with breast implants," Emma said quickly.

Traffic murmured behind us. "Sure is hot," Pete said.

The Doctor Is OUT (Hour of the Break and Enter)

I got out of the truck and surveyed the strip mall. "Looks like there's a second story. I bet Parkinson's office is up there." I made for a set of exterior stairs at one corner of the mall. My clogs clip-clacked embarrassingly and the hot air shimmering off the black asphalt made the hem of my frilly apron flutter. My hands and face felt sweaty, although that might have been nerves.

A small walkway, like the one on the second story of a motel, led past a bunch of shabby professional offices on the upper floor. There was an accountant with an Out of Business sign on the door, and a travel agency announcing "We Specialize in Serving the Elderly!"—presumably because everybody not confined to a wheelchair had figured out how to buy their own airplane tickets online. In classic California fashion, there were not one but two chiropractors, a dietician, an acupuncturist, and the Herbal Hut *(Vitamins, Mineral Supplements, and More Than Twenty Varieties of Bottled Water!!!)*.

But finally, there it was.

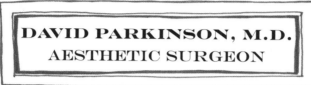

DAVID PARKINSON, M.D.
AESTHETIC SURGEON

"Kind of dim inside," Emma muttered, peering through the glass.

I turned sideways, looking at my reflection in the dark door. "Do you really think my butt is too flat?"

"I don't think it's open," Pete said.

I pushed the puffy sleeves of my peasant blouse back to my elbows, took a deep breath, and walked in. Pete was half right about the office being closed. The door was unlocked, but the office inside seemed to be empty. No patients lounged in the comfy chairs in the small waiting room or flipped through the copies of *Golf Digest* on the coffee table. No receptionist sat behind the tiny reception desk. The only living things were the fish flicking through the aquarium that sat, glowing and blue, against one wall. The light over the reception desk was on, but the one in the waiting area was off, so you could see faint gleams and ripples of light from the aquarium playing over the dull beige carpet.

53.

I walked up to the reception desk. "Hello?" No answer. On the counter there was a sign-in sheet and a bell. I rang the bell—*ting!* The nervous feeling in my stomach changed, as if I were in a movie and the background music had just switched into a sinister minor key.

"Nobody home," Pete said. I rang the bell again. Nothing.

Just to the right of the reception desk, a small door led to what I presumed would be the consulting room. "I'm going to see if anyone is back there," I said quietly. "Emma, if you watch the front door, maybe Pete could take a look at the computer?" Pete nodded.

"Wait," Emma said. She walked in front of me and pulled open the door to the consulting room. "Fingerprints," she said. "The police have yours on file, remember?"

Weird, but true. One set of cops had nearly caught me breaking into Victor's house and then kidnapped me later. I'd even had some fingerprints taken—as a precaution, of course—by the second set of police, the ones who charged in like the cavalry and rescued me and Victor, thanks to a bit of quick thinking by Emma. I owe that girl a lot. "Thanks," I said.

Beyond the door was a small consulting room. The basic furnishings could have come from any doctor's office anywhere: one of those vinyl-covered examination tables with the paper covers on it, a blood pressure monitor, a cabinet with the usual inventory of tongue depressors, cotton swabs, and latex gloves. There were some other things, though, that reminded you that this was a plastic surgeon's office. Tons of mirrors, for one thing, and between the mirrors a series of Before and After pictures of Dr. Parkinson's clients. The "Before" men were pudgy and balding; the "After" ones had more hair, big toothy smiles, and six-pack abs. Presumably Dr. Parkinson was promising a metamorphosis, but I got the feeling the poor Before guys had been lured into a spaceship and thrown into a recycling vat, while back on Earth they were replaced with cunningly sculpted clones that were the first gambit for an alien takeover of the earth.

As for the women … One thing you learn, if you draw a lot of portraits, is that as far as the pencil is concerned, age and gravity are basically the same thing. This is what happens to women: we sag. Our boobs droop and our ankles get thick, as extra weight slowly pools at the bottom of our legs. Some of us get little pot bellies low down on our abdomens. The little bit of rather attractive fat in the hollows above our eyes mysteriously moves down to become extra chins, or jowls, or even wattles, if we are unlucky. But the happy "After" women in these photographs had tight, perky faces and big perky boobs that bravely ignored gravity and looked as if they would do so perpetually if only the women could keep smiling. Looking around at those photographs I realized it wasn't just beauty the good doctor was selling. It was youth.

In the background I could hear Emma and Pete talking quietly and moving around the reception area. I tried another "hello" and got more silence back, so I headed to the door at the back of the consulting room. I stuck my hand under my Swiss peasant blouse and turned the doorknob through the cloth so I wouldn't leave any fingerprints.

The room beyond was some kind of lab or dispensary, small and cluttered. The first thing I noticed was the smell of rubbing alcohol. The second was the body on the floor. My heart flipped in my chest. It was Dr. Parkinson. I recognized him from the day my father had died and he "happened" to be dropping by. He was lying slumped against a wall with his head lolling to one side and his eyes closed. For one eternal instant I was sure he was dead.

Then a thin silver thread of drool trickled from his mouth and I saw his eyes roll slowly under their closed lids. Not dead, then, but sleeping. I held my breath, wondering if we could technically be charged with breaking and entering, given that the front door was unlocked. My heart was going like a jackhammer. I was amazed that the sound of it thudding against my ribs didn't wake Parkinson up, but he just lay there, completely inert. He was wearing a lab coat over pants and his shirt was rumpled. On his right foot he wore brown socks and a loafer, but his left foot was bare. The left shoe was lying next to a set of metal filing cabinets, with the sock tucked inside. The naked foot seemed shockingly pale and vulnerable. There were little swirls of hair around the knuckle of his big toe; I could imagine exactly how I would draw them.

"Excuse me?" I whispered. "Are you okay?"

Not so much as an eyelid twitch.

I got a little bolder. "Hey," I said, in my regular voice. "Doctor, doctor. Code blue on the dispensary floor."

Nothing.

I noticed he had what looked like a medical ID bracelet around his wrist, but when I crouched down to read it all it said was "r3m3mb3r."

Hmm. I went back to the waiting area and locked the front door from the inside so we wouldn't be disturbed. "Uh—guys? Could you come in here for a minute?"

Moments later, the three of us edged into the back room.

Once again I noticed the tang of rubbing alcohol in the air. It reminded me of biology class and frogs pickled in formaldehyde. "I'm not sure what to do," I said, gesturing at the body lolling on the floor. "It's like he's in a coma or something."

Pete crouched down by the body. "If he's had a stroke, we have to get him to a hospital right away," Pete said, feeling for a pulse. He frowned, then pulled one eyelid open. Parkinson gurgled but remained limp. Pete looked back over his shoulder, grinning. "I don't think he's had a stroke," he said. "Dude is just seriously *stoned*." He looked around, saw a little metal trash can nearby, and sifted through it. "Yep," he said, holding up a small disposable syringe. "Ladies and gentlemen, The Doctor Is Out."

"*Glj forble*," Parkinson added. "*Mmvoop*."

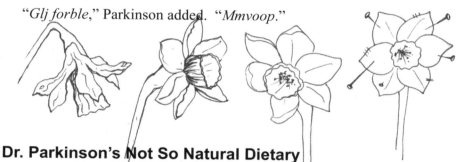

Dr. Parkinson's Not So Natural Dietary Supplement (Hour of the Instant Vacation)

"That's why there's no receptionist," Emma said. "He sent her home so he could party in the back room."

"Or she called in sick so he decided to take the day off in dreamland," I said.

"I still don't understand why he has one shoe off," Emma asked.

"He was shooting up between his toes," I guessed, remembering something my mom had told me. "The needle tracks—you want to put the needle somewhere nobody will see the mark." The syringe also explained the smell of rubbing alcohol. I imagined him swabbing it between his toes, disinfecting the area where he meant to shoot up. *Eew.*

"So this would have been his workroom," Emma said, looking around. "I guess he did actual surgery somewhere else." She sidled over to one of the cabinets and peeked at the bottles there. "Vitamins. Dietary supplements. Lots of painkillers ... Codeine. Vicodin. Valium," she read. "I wonder if he was prescribing drugs for himself."

"Doesn't look like this guy was living large," Pete said. The whole office had a small, shabby feeling to it, but this back room was really a mess—a jumble of pill bottles in the cabinets, a few dirty dishes in the sink and empty beer bottles dotting the counter space. Next to the sink was a small microwave with a Cup O' Soup still standing inside it. And of course Dr. Parkinson himself, poured out on the floor like something that had spilled out of a milkshake cup.

Emma scratched her hair. "So ... what do we do now?"

"Well, we came here to find out some things about my dad." I looked at Pete. "How's it going with the computers?"

He grimaced. "Not great. Dude's got a biometric password system set up. A fingerprint scanner," he translated, seeing my blank look. "Pretty advanced security for a place like this. This guy must have stuff he really doesn't want anyone to see."

"So you can't just get in with cyber-voodoo or something?"

"I sniffed around to see if he had a wireless router I could hack, but no luck." Pete shrugged. "No fingerprint, no access."

I looked back at Parkinson. "*Ffrrp,*" he mumbled. A little bubble formed between his lips and then popped. "*Gorzzzz.*"

My eyes narrowed. "I have an idea."

"Oh," Emma said. "Please don't."

"We carry him into reception and hold his finger down on the scanning plate." Pete looked intrigued. Emma looked appalled, but then I was pretty used to that. "Come on," I said, "give me a hand lugging this guy. I'll take the head."

"*Glik*," Parkinson sighed. "*Gug. Ploof.*"

Dr. Parkinson Lends A Hand

Parkinson wasn't a particularly big man, and he certainly wasn't struggling, but carting him out to the reception area was surprisingly difficult. It was like trying to carry a hundred and seventy pounds of limp spaghetti. Pete had the legs, while Emma and I struggled with the torso.

"Pete, his legs are sliding!" Emma yelped. "Can't you—"

"You just watch out for the—" *WHACK!* "—head getting through the doorway," Pete finished unnecessarily.

Emma hovered unhappily over the doctor's drooling face. "Do you think we broke his nose?"

"If we did, he can always fix it up," I said callously. "I'm sure he'd give himself a discount." I snarled in frustration. "Arg! His stupid arm keeps getting tangled in my frilly apron."

"I think we'll have to turn him sideways, like an armchair," Pete puffed, after our second attempt to get Parkinson through the door had ended in disaster.

"Good idea," I grunted.

"I help a lot of friends move," he said. "That's what happens when you're—"

"The guy with the truck," I finished, as we tipped Parkinson over on his side. The little silver thread of drool stretched behind him like a slug track. Emma struggled to change her grip and dropped him by accident so his face bounced onto the floor with a damp thud, like a cantaloupe rolling off a coffee table.

"*Mph!*" he mused thickly into the carpet. "*Shullllg.*"

"Sorry!" Emma squeaked.

"Jeez, this dude is heavy," Pete panted, angling around so we could make it through the door into the reception area.

Unfortunately, just getting Parkinson near the computer didn't mean we had solved all our problems. We tried sitting his limp body in the receptionist's chair, but that was like starting a Slinky down a flight of stairs, a long liquid folding and sliding that ended up with Parkinson wrapped improbably around the base of the swivel chair.

"Let's just leave him there," I said, breathing heavily. "We only need his hand anyway. Pete, grab his finger."

"Uh, I'm just an employee," Pete said, looking at Emma. "You're the boss."

Emma took a deep breath but I cut her off. "Fine, I'll do it." I grabbed Parkinson's hand, which was warm and floppy. "Which finger?"

"Try the index finger on the right hand—that's pretty common."

"Okay." Parkinson's finger was as limp and rubbery as a carrot left in the fridge too long. I tugged it over to the computer and slid it repeatedly across the scanner. On the fifth try it worked, and a menu system bloomed on the screen. "Bingo!" Pete said, starting to click his way through it.

Momentarily unattended, Parkinson trickled slowly out of the chair and onto the floor again. Emma and I exchanged desperate looks. "We could try dragging him back to the dispensary while Pete is working," Emma said tentatively.

"Or we could stuff him under the desk until Pete is done."

"I second that motion," she said. It was but the work of a minute to wedge the doctor securely under the desk. "Okay," Emma said. "I'm going to go back to that workroom. I thought I saw something like a lab book—it might be worth a look."

She headed back and I stayed to hover over Pete's shoulder, watching as he dug deeper and deeper into Dr. Parkinson's files. "Vickers," I said. "Michael Vickers."

"Nope. Nada." He frowned. "Hang on … Let's ask about hidden files…"

And then, there it was—**Vickers, M.** Pete clicked. A screen came up with a picture of my father.

It was the first time I had seen even a picture of him in more than a year. My mom had boxed up all the photographs of my father and put them in the garage. *It's time to get on with our lives*, she had said, but I think the real reason was they made her too sad. I used to sneak out to the garage and look through the box, but it made me sad, too, and then the whole business with Victor had started up and I had been so busy … I felt a terrible shock of guilt, thinking of those photographs out in the garage, gathering dust. As if I had forgotten him already. As if I didn't care.

"Hunh. That's funny," Pete murmured. He clicked a link marked **Chan, Victor**—*what?!?*—and a second window opened on the screen. This was a file about Victor, and at the very top of the page was a picture of him talking to Jun, Ancestor Lu's estranged daughter. The two of them were so close their heads were touching, as if they were sharing a secret, or a private joke.

At that moment, someone banged on Dr. Parkinson's door.

61.

Vickers' Field Guide
To Immortals of Northern California

Ancestor Lu
(Immortalitatus grantor)
One of the Eight Immortals of Chinese
Taoism. Thinks he wants to give everyone
the secret to eternal life; actually just wants
to save one very mortal daughter... much
to the irritation of his other daughter,
the very immortal

Jun
(Feline infernus)
Lu's estranged daughter believes her dad is
going through his Mid-Eternity Crisis and is
bringing dishonor on their house by lying,
cheating, and murdering anyone who tries to
keep him from being the Nicest Guy Ever.
Generally thought to have her eye on

62.

Victor
(Amorus absentia)
The amazing disappearing boyfriend. Currently
working WITH Ancestor Lu to find the key to
immortality in exchange for Lu not crushing me like a
bug. Recently revealed as the son of

Tsao Kuo Ch'iu

(Amorus compulsivus)

Another one of the Eight Chinese Immortals, only with a crush on me—his son's GF. (Eww.) Thinks most humans = head lice. Utterly opposed to Ancestor Lu's Get Immortal Quick scheme, making him natural ally of

Paper Folding Man (aka Chang Kuo-Lao)

(Meddlus inscrutabilis)

Rides donkey backward and folds him up like a map. How do you trust a guy like that? Unclear whether he is for or against Lu. In this way, similar to

Auntie Joe (aka The Fortune Teller)

(Grumpimus omnivisor)

Not native to the area, but may have been blown off course during migration. Immortal AND precognitive; runs a string of fortune-telling businesses themed for different markets (Chinese, voodoo, Gypsy, etc.) Seems to be looking out for me. Genetic note: not Chinese, suggesting immortality not confined to one racial group. Disliked by anyone with secrets.

63.

A Heck of a Racket (Hour of Slutty Heidi's Alpenhorn)

I straightened up as if electrocuted, just in time to see a forty-year-old woman in tennis whites whacking the glass door with a racket. "Open this door!"

I stared under the desk. Dr. Parkinson's eyelids snapped open, but then his eyeballs rolled back in his head one at a time—first the left, then the right.

"Uh-oh," Pete said.

"Don't worry," I said. "I have everything under control."

I walked out from behind the desk with my best professional smile and waved at Tennis Lady through the door. "I'm sorry, we're closed!" I yelled. "Would you like to reschedule?"

Her gaze raked witheringly across me. "Who are you? Little Bo Peep? Reschedule my ass. Open this door."

I cocked my head as if I was having trouble hearing her, although in fact I was pretty sure she could be heard from San Jose to the Golden Gate Bridge. She had the kind of voice that could stop a seventh grade class in its tracks, or make beauty salon technicians whimper with fear. I tapped my imaginary wristwatch. "Sorry, we're closed!"

"You're closed? Closed? Okay." She took out her cell phone. "I'm calling the police."

"No!" I squeaked. "I mean, why?"

She flipped the phone open and punched in the first number. "Nine…"

"The *police?* Are you crazy? You can't call the police just because you want an appoint—"

"One…" she said implacably, punching another key.

"Fine!" I unlocked the door and jerked it open. "Come in already."

Tennis Lady closed her phone and stalked inside with the satisfied look of a polar bear advancing on a baby seal. "What happened to the other receptionist? Or does he just get easily tired of women who are old enough to drive?"

"My name is, uh—my name is Jewel," I said. "I'm helping out with reception today. This is Chad, our computer guy."

The Valkyrie gave Pete a smile that would strike fear into the hearts of pool boys and pizza delivery guys everywhere. "Hi, Chad," she said.

She turned back and tapped me lightly on the collarbone with her tennis racket. "What's with the Slutty Heidi outfit?"

"Good question," I said idiotically.

"Folk dancing," Pete said.

"What?"

"You were on your way to your folk dancing class."

"I've never heard of Swiss folk dancing," Tennis Lady said suspiciously.

"You haven't?" I said, trying to sound surprised. "Oh, yes, the Swiss are extremely musical. Think of glockenspiels, for instance, and, and . . . "

"Alpenhorns," Pete said.

"Exactly. As a matter of fact," I continued, "I was just on the way to a recital. My folk dancing club is performing at a senior center very soon, so I'm afraid I don't have time to—"

Tennis Lady was apparently unbothered by the idea that she might be depriving senior citizens of the joy of my clog-clacking interpretative dance skills. "Where the hell is Dr. Parkinson?"

I heard a faint, fearful "*Gloog!*" from under the reception desk. "I'm so sorry, but Dr. Parkinson is not available at the moment. Can I take a message?"

66.

"Message. My. Ass." The Soccer Mom from Hell tapped my collarbone with her tennis racket again. "It was his idea to get together for drinks. He was the one who suggested that I could 'earn a discount' on the procedure." Tennis Lady gave me a little shove with the tennis racket. "The trouble with trying to make a little extra money—<shove>—by threatening to send pictures to my husband—<shove>—is that it assumes my husband gives a damn."

"Could you possibly stop hitting me with your tennis racket?" I said.

"Shut up. Now you find Parkinson, and you give him that message from me," Tennis Lady said. "And you can tell him that if I am not one hundred percent satisfied, I will be reporting him to the police for blackmail."

"Well, I'll just be giving him that message, then," I babbled. "And I guarantee you won't be disappointed." I sidled back around the reception desk. "Dr. Parkinson is the best. Award-winning. Did you know that? He was voted Aesthetic Surgeon of the Year for Silicone Valley." Tennis Lady narrowed her eyes. "Silicon Valley, I mean." Under the desk, the good doctor was beginning to curl and pulse like a jellyfish in a microwave. "He can make anyone look young. Youn*ger*," I added hastily.

The door to the consulting room opened and Emma peered out. "What's going on out here?"

"Who the hell is she?" Tennis Lady demanded.

"A patient," I said brightly. "In fact, Miss Cheung here is thirty-five years old."

Tennis Lady stared at Emma. "Thirty-five?"

"Thirty-five!" Emma blurted. She glared at me, then

swallowed. "Not quite. My, uh, my birthday's not for another month."

I looked at Emma and said "thank you" a thousand times with my eyes. She stared and said "you owe me" a thousand times back.

"Thirty-four. Whatever," Tennis Lady said, examining Emma with new appreciation. "Maybe Parkinson's as good as he says he is." She reached up and actually touched the skin of Emma's face as if testing the thread count on an expensive sheet. "I mean, I know you people age well, but—"

"Impressive, isn't it?" I said, before Emma could quite figure out what she meant by that. "Anyway, I'll give the doctor your message," I said, looking perkily at the door.

"I think I'll give it to him myself," Tennis Lady purred.

"I'm afraid I don't know exactly when he'll be back."

"I'll wait," she said.

I was beginning to think her husband had run off with my secret twin and she was going to dedicate the rest of her life to making me suffer.

"I'll just print out those files," Pete said.

"Files?"

"For Ms. Cheung," Pete said. He flicked his eyes at the screen, and I saw the two open files, one on Victor and one on my dad.

"Oh, right. Those files."

The five of us waited in the office together: Tennis Lady and Emma in the waiting room. Pete hovering by the printer. Me behind the desk. Dr. Parkinson under it.

A fly buzzed in the room. Tennis Lady killed it with her racket.

67.

Time passed.

"Okay," Pete said. "I think that's it."

"Are you all done?" I said brightly. Nodding.

"I … think so," he said, watching me. "Here are the files."

"Great!" I took the pages and rolled them up into a tube and remembered to hand them to Emma. "Well, the senior citizens are waiting," I said.

Tennis Lady smiled wolfishly. "Knock 'em dead, honey. I'll just wait here."

Emma started slowly for the door, and after a moment's hesitation, Pete followed her. "Gee," I said. "That's nice of you. I guess I'll be off, then." I started to come out from around the desk, but something caught my foot and I tripped. Dr. Parkinson's hand was wrapped around my ankle. He was looking a good deal more conscious now, and some dim species of alarm was swimming over his face. *"Boof?"* he mumbled. *"Zorp?"*

"Did you hear someone talking?" Tennis Lady said suspiciously. She looked at the door into the consulting room and her eyes narrowed. "Is there a back entrance into this place?"

"Maybe," I said loudly, kicking free of Parkinson's twitching fingers. "Maybe you should check out the room in the back." Tennis Lady stepped menacingly toward the consultation room as I edged around the desk, making sure to stay out of range of her racket. "Good luck finding Dr. Parkinson," I said, pulling open the front door. "It sounds like you guys have a lot to talk about."

"Gilp!" said a mournful voice behind me. Then I was outside the office with my clogs chattering across the asphalt and my frilly apron whipping around my legs as I sprinted for the truck.

Dinosaurs of Silicon Valley (Hour of the Cathy 30/30 Plan)

Pete drove. I pored over the documents we had printed off Dr. Parkinson's computer. Emma complained. "Honestly, Cathy, I'm beginning to think the four most terrifying words in the English language are 'I have an idea!'"

"Hypothermia a good start?" I read. *"Thorazine might stop shivers.* Do you know what Thorazine is?"

"It's the Cathy Vickers thirty–thirty plan," Emma continued, paying no attention to me at all. "Thirty criminal charges and thirty years in jail."

"Inderal or equiv induce bradycardia," I read. "Wasn't Bradycardia the dinosaur with the funny head?"

"You mean Brachiosauros?" Pete said. "I thought that was the one with the spiny fin on its back."

"Plus now we know Parkinson is definitely a blackmailer!" Emma pointed out. "What if there was a security camera filming that whole ridiculous escapade? Every time I put out a press release or buy another company I'll be checking my mailbox for one of those extortion notes where they cut the words out of letters in a magazine."

"I thought that was ransom notes," Pete said.

"You stay out of this. And it's Lambeosaurus that has the bumps on its head," she added.

"I guess it wouldn't make much sense for Parkinson to be talking about dinosaurs," I muttered, still trying to puzzle my way through the medical notes on my father's file.

"Maybe he was injecting your dad with dinosaur DNA, like in *Jurassic Park*," Pete suggested.

Emma gave him a look that dried him up like a blob of spit

69.

on a hot sidewalk. "Just drive us home," she said.

"Oh," I said. "Here's a word I recognize." There must have been something about my tone of voice, because Emma cut herself off in mid-complaint. I met her eyes. *"Curare,"* I said. "As in the poison."

She swallowed. "Can I see?"

I handed over the printouts. "I think this whole file is about one thing: how to poison my dad." And to my shame I noticed, mixed with the horror, a tiny feeling of relief. If my dad had been murdered, I would move heaven and earth to find out who had done it, and make them pay. But Jewel was right: there was a part of me that would rather find out my father had been murdered than discover he had walked out on us of his own free will.

Microwave Tamales (Hour of the Unwanted Guests)

Under a hundred-year-old treaty, Hong Kong was due to return to the control of mainland China in 1997. The businessmen of HK began stashing their families on the West Coast of the U.S. in the late 80s and early 90s in case life under the Communists turned out to be unbearable. By the time Mr. Cheung sent Emma to America, it had become almost the trendy thing to do in his circle. Because of their habit of flying back and forth from China to America every couple of weeks, parents like Mr. Cheung were called "astronauts," although Emma's dad had been too busy with his business deals to rack up many frequent-flier miles coming to California. Emma had left her Very British private school shortly after turning thirteen, showing up at Burlingame Middle School for eighth grade. At the time,

Emma's dad had been pretty flush, and her apartment was a big place in a nice building, with the sort of expensive leather-covered furniture that had been all the rage in about 1983.

About the same time I figured out that Victor was immortal, Mr. Cheung had turned up on Emma's doorstep, bankrupt and one step ahead of some very nasty creditors. For a while it had looked as if they would probably be living out of a bus shelter in a month. My would-be stalker, Tsao, had stepped in at the eleventh hour as an investor in DoubleTalk Wireless, the company Emma had started in order to capture part of the Chinese cell phone market. He had become her business mentor, and even offered to buy Emma and her dad a condo, but that didn't sit well with Emma's pride. Instead she traded him some stock in DoubleTalk—retaining majority control, of course—and negotiated a small salary for herself as president of the company. The money was just enough to pay the rent on the apartment, lease her beloved BMW, and allow her and her father to live modestly while she put herself through business school at Berkeley.

As we made our way up to Emma's apartment, I was trying to think of how to get rid of Pete. He seemed like a nice guy, and he had just risked criminal prosecution on my behalf, but I certainly wasn't going to talk about My Life Among the Immortals in front of him. Frankly, I was dying to get rid of him so that Emma and I could talk openly. But as soon as Emma's apartment door swung open, I realized our heart-to-heart talk would have to wait. The table was set for three, Tsao was sitting at it, and Emma's dad was just bustling in from the kitchen with a tray full of steaming-hot microwave tamales. "Emma! Just right time," he beamed. Then his eye fell on me and his smile deflated.

71.

www.doubletalkwireless.com

"Hey," Pete said.

Mr. Cheung's smile disappeared entirely, to be replaced by that expression you get when you notice there are weevils swimming in your cereal bowl. "So sorry, family small dinner!" Mr. Cheung said briefly, not sounding sorry at all.

"We can always microwave a few more tamales." Emma smiled at Tsao. "This is a lovely surprise!"

"Cathy," Tsao said, dipping his head, the faintest suggestion of a bow. "A lovely surprise indeed." Like Emma, his accent was Oxford and impeccable; his suit was Armani and equally above reproach. It was depressingly clear from Emma's expression that she was crazy about the guy. And why not? He was more than a thousand years old, it was true, but he didn't look a day over thirty. He was sophisticated, well educated, powerful, and (let's face it) rich. Basically, Tsao was exactly who Emma wanted to be.

Or … my eyes flicked to her father, who was wearing his one remaining pinstriped suit, brushed within an inch of its life. Tsao wasn't just Emma's role model. He was what she had always needed her *father* to be.

Let's face it: Emma's dad had abandoned her. The only way for her to make that right in her own head was to believe that he was someone amazing, a godlike figure striding the corridors of high finance. The bigger he was, the more her sacrifice would have been part of something bigger, something grand. When Mr. Cheung showed up at her door, just another bad-luck businessman…

I had dropped by her place the day before graduation. Mr. Cheung was excited about the whole thing; he was out renting himself a tuxedo for the big ceremony. I found Emma in her room. She was sitting in the middle of her bed with all her assignments around her: English and math and geography and social studies, folder after folder, everything back to eighth grade, A+, A+, A+, A, A+... None of them had ever been read or seen or admired—just turned in, graded, brought back to the empty apartment and filed away. Now they were spread out on the bed like insect husks, like last year's brittle leaves. Emma's head was in her hands, her face expressionless.

I went into the kitchen and microwaved a mini pizza for her. By the time the food was ready her room was immaculate, all five years of homework neatly filed away. After we ate I dragged her back to my house to watch videos. When Mr. Cheung returned to their apartment, eager to show off his tuxedo, he was surprised to find himself alone.

Thinking back, Emma had been due for a crash of monumental proportions. Instead, *hey presto!* Tsao showed up like the white knight in a fairy tale, and all the allegiance Emma once had to her father could be transferred to a man who truly was the demigod of her fantasies.

The demigod now surveyed my Fondue! waitress outfit with a glimmer of amusement. "That ensemble is very..."

"It is, isn't it?" I said, wishing the frilly apron was a little less frilly and the short skirt not quite so short.

"Cathy dress crazy," Emma's dad said. "My Emma more respectable."

"Oh, I think it's all right if a young woman is a little less than respectable every now and again." Tsao smiled. "Mr. Cheung, I'm sure we can make room for a couple more guests," he added, indicating the empty chair next to his. He said something in Chinese, and he and Mr. Cheung had a brief,

73.

polite disagreement that I suspected went something like:

"How nice! Cathy and a young man. Please, allow me to order in food."

"Oh, I couldn't possibly. The young man is wanted for arson, and I hear Cathy has lice."

"Allow me to remind you that I could buy Lichtenstein."

"But—"

And then Tsao smashed his fist on the table so hard the silverware chattered. "Damn it, I *pay* you!" he shouted.

Dead silence. I had never, ever heard Tsao lose his temper. A man who has lived a thousand years doesn't get easily upset. Everyone looked shocked, Tsao most of all. "F-forgive me," he said. "I have been oddly temperamental of late. Something . . ." He gave me the strangest look, then, hungry and haunted at the same time. "Something has upset my equilibrium."

> *Tsao saw her one day in the*
> *marketplace, and her glance*
> *passed through his heart like an*
> *arrow: the breath and life struck*
> *from him in an instant, and the*
> *sound of the bowstring still*
> *humming.*

In the old stories of the Eight Immortals, it was said that Tsao Kuo Ch'iu, distraught at having murdered the woman he loved and her husband, had run into the mountains, renouncing all worldly things to study the Tao. There, legend says he met Ancestor Lu, who gave him the secret of eternal life. But Victor had said the immortal gene was only triggered by imminent death. I found myself imagining Tsao looking down at the blood-spattered body of his slaughtered love, seeing the knife that had killed her clenched in his hand. I could see him wiping the slippery red handle to get a better grip and then plunging it into his own heart, desperate to end his life—but damning himself instead to a love-haunted eternity.

Mr. Cheung fluttered his hands and made to soothe his important guest. "Stress!" he said. "Work, work, work! Is doing business. Quiet family dinner, yes, what you need!" He turned a short burst of Chinese on Emma.

"A dress?" she said, surprised. "Isn't that a bit fancy for nuked tamales?" She waved at her standard summer outfit of T-shirt and jeans. "What's wrong with this?"

"I think you look fine," Pete said.

Mr. Cheung shot me a desperate glance.

Oh.

This wasn't a business dinner to Emma's dad. This was a *date*. He was trying to set her up with Tsao. That explained the sour look on his face when Pete drifted across his threshold. Emma had no clue Pete was interested in anything but stock options in DoubleTalk, but her dad was not quite so dumb. He knew a rival when he saw one. *And a meal ticket, too,* I thought, glancing back at Tsao.

Gross.

But of course it made eight kinds of sense. Why risk Tsao and Tsao's lovely money disappearing if DoubleTalk didn't get off the ground? Why have a rich investor when you could have a rich son-in-law instead?

Mr. Cheung was still looking at me. "So sorry," he said. "I know Emma has been good friend to you." Translation: *please don't screw this up for her. For once.*

Tsao stood up to offer me a chair. "You know, I should be getting home," I said.

Emma looked down at the roll of computer printouts still in her hand. "Uh…"

"We'll talk later," I said.

Tsao's eyes flicked almost imperceptibly over at Emma's dad, then back to me. "This is … disappointing," he remarked. "Perhaps another time?"

"Yeah, well—work, you know. Busy, busy," I said. "I better go before I miss my bus."

"Oh, Pete can give you a ride home," Emma said casually. "You can drop her off, can't you, Pete?"

Pete looked from Emma to Mr. Cheung. "Uh, yeah," he said, with a touch of irony that everyone but Emma could hear. "I can do that."

Pete (Hour of Surveillance by People from the Future)

Pete drove with one hand on the wheel, the other absently tapping out a rhythm on the truck seat, and one foot jiggling as we pulled out of the parking lot behind Emma's building. "Hey, I'm sorry about your dad," he said.

"Thanks."

It was the middle of summer, and the grass on the side of the road had long since turned to straw and dust. It was after seven, the time painters call "the magic hour," when the slanting light turns clear and golden and everything you look at feels like a memory.

"Emma told me you and your father were real close. I

spent a lot of time with my dad, too," Pete said. "He was an engineer. Civilian, but he worked with the Navy all the time. Sonar and radar and stuff. We mostly lived on or near naval bases. Every Saturday we used to go out to the landfill and scavenge for parts. We were always building things. Battle-bots! I was huge into that when I was a kid."

"Rock 'em Sock 'em Robots?"

"Yeah, but making your own and then fighting them with remotes."

"It's hard to believe boys are part of the same species," I said. "You guys seem only distantly related to us, like orangutans or lemurs or something."

Pete laughed. "When I was little I used to collect mercury."

"Mercury?"

"Yeah, you can find a lot in a dump. Lots of appliances use mercury switches. Lights, for instance, and a lot of gas stoves, too; a lot of times there's a mercury switch that controls the flow of gas at the pilot light so that—never mind. You don't care. The point is, I had this big glob of mercury. Have you ever played with it? The coolest stuff ever."

"Isn't it poisonous?"

Pete shrugged. "Well, I didn't eat it."

"I thought it made you crazy."

"Well, sure, but not in a *bad* way," he said, grinning. "Anyway, the rest of my family is crazy as it is."

To the east, the hills behind San Jose had turned the color of a lion's pelt, a tawny ridgeline against the blue sky. "We have some funny ones, too," I said. "My mom's Uncle Mort has a collection of vegetables shaped like U.S. presidents. Though to be fair, the beet does look a *lot* like Bill Clinton."

"My dad thinks he's being watched by people from the future." Pete didn't stop smiling, but from the way he said it I knew he wasn't kidding. He wasn't talking about a dad who was eccentric. He was talking about growing up with a father who was genuinely not living in the same world as the rest of us.

"That sounds … scary."

Pete shrugged, smiling. "Sonar and radar, right? He was convinced that the Future People were spying on him with advanced technology. Most of his research actually comes from trying to escape from the Future People."

"Wow," I said. "What did your mom say about that?"

"Oh, they divorced when I was real little."

"And your dad got custody?"

He gave me a sideways look. "The court decided Mom wasn't stable enough to raise kids."

As opposed to the man who was under surveillance by aliens. "Ouch."

"No big," he said. "It was a long time ago."

We approached my exit and got off the freeway. I watched Pete drive. His eyes were very alert, always glancing around, his fingers tapping, his foot jiggling. *Radar,* I thought. *Always scanning for the next sign of trouble.* "So how did you meet up with Emma?" I asked.

"She put an ad online looking for programmers and I answered." He laughed. "It turned out she wanted to pay in shares of a nonexistent company, so there wasn't much competition for the job."

"Why did you take it?"

"I like to hang out with people smarter than I am."

"Okay, but you have to pay the rent, too. Emma should at least get Tsao to cover—"

"I don't need any of that guy's money," Pete said curtly.
My eyebrows rose. "That's okay—he'll be gone as soon as
DoubleTalk goes under and then we can build a real company."

"You don't think DoubleTalk will work?"

"It's the Chinese cell phone market," Pete said patiently.
"Every big player in the wireless world has an army of
engineers and marketers trying to get in there. To make it, you
need an idea that the big boys haven't already had."

Somehow, it had never occurred to me that Emma's business
plans would be anything but perfect, even if she was just out of
high school. "Have you shared this analysis with Emma?"

"Nah. She'll figure it out. She's smart."

"If she's so smart, why did she come up with the crazy
China plan in the first place?" I said.

Pete rolled to a stop in front of my house. "She was
fifteen," he said. "And her dad was over there."

I looked at him. "For a guy who builds battle-bots for fun,
you aren't so dumb."

"When I was growing up, we were really poor," Pete said.
"One year I had a paper route through a rich neighborhood. I
always wanted money, but the people on that paper route sucked.
I'd see them living in their big houses and making a zillion dollars
and I could tell they didn't have a clue. They were like him."

"Tsao?"

"Yeah. To most rich people, money is power." I opened
the door and got out of the truck. "That's what's cool about
Emma," Pete said. "She's totally into money, but she isn't like
that at all. Money isn't power to her."

"What is it?"

He thought about it for a second, then grinned. "Lego," he said.

79.

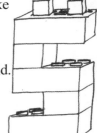

To: victor
Cc:

Subject: broke & lonely—thanks for asking

Attachments: none

Verdana — 14 — **B** *I* U T

Hey dummy—

Answer my damn email already. Some of us don't have a thousand years to wait.

So we went over to see this guy, David "Better Living Through Breast Enhancement" Parkinson. Turned out he had a file on my dad, full of notes on how to poison him. Funny thing is, he had a file on you, too. With pictures. And he knew you wouldn't die.

Victor, I'm beginning to feel like the deaf kid in a game of musical chairs. It's hard to believe you're on my side if you don't pick up the phone when I call or answer my emails when I write. I'm going for my 4th crappy job of the summer (speaking of which, you could at least reimburse me for my Burger Barn salary!) Not to be a gold digger, but I got nothing. I'm not like Emma. I'm going to be working as a waitress when I'm 60. And it's not like you're gonna be around then, right? You'll still be 23 or so, with your pick of all the cute young girls, although I should warn you I have no problem beating those young floozies to death with my walker. Or who knows, maybe you like older women and find false teeth erotic.

I'm tired of you never answering my emails, Victor. Give me a reason to believe in you. In us.

C

Be careful what you wish for!

80.

Broke and Lonely (Hour of the Unfortunate Email)

I checked my email as soon as I got home. Three more messages from Tsao, which I deleted unread. Nothing from Victor. Again.

Next Day: The Continuing Adventures of FondueGirl!

The lunch rush was picking up. Six tables in my section and Nora the Chain-Smoking Hostess was showing a fussy-looking businesswoman over to Table 13. I tried my best Swiss Ninja Death Glare to make Nora seat her in Todd's section, but the Fondue! uniform for male waiters involved very short shorts and lederhosen. Todd was a great guy, but he was both heavily tattooed and kinda furry. The effect was a bit overwhelming in lederhosen, so Nora never seated single women in Todd's section. Or children. Or people with heart conditions or pacemakers or the elderly in general.

I clogged into my section, struggling to smile under my tray, which held Table 4's "Sizzling Mixed Meat Fondue for Two." For those of you who skipped the prerequisite courses, fondue comes in three basic varieties. There's the kind you thought of first, where you dip cubes of bread into a pot of cheese. There's chocolate fondue, which is a dessert thing where you dip strawberries or orange slices or pear cubes into a pot of warm chocolate. But there is also meat fondue, the most dangerous of all the fondues when encountered in the wild. Meat fondue was invented by Swiss people being besieged in castles during feudal times. As everybody knows, medieval people thought about the funnest thing in the world was to pour

Love doesn't grow on trees.

81.

Fondue Girl!

82.

boiling oil on armored men trying to get into your castle. Well, when a siege had dragged on long enough for hunger to set in, the Swiss got in the habit of grabbing passing rats and dipping them into the oil for a snack.

At Fondue! they didn't have rat on the menu (well, not officially, but honestly, how would you tell?). We pretty much stuck to beef, chicken, and pork, but the boiling oil was still there, and every bit as dangerous as it was in the old days. Given that it was my second day on the job and I wasn't totally steady in my Alpen Clogs, I was very careful as I sidled over to Table 4.

I had mentally tagged the two guys waiting for their Mixed Meat entrée as Beef and Pork. Beef was friendly and huge and built like a weightlifter. Pork was friendly and short and built like a beanbag chair.

"Here you go," I said, flashing my best Perky Waitress smile and trying to inch the serving platter off my shoulder.

The Blackberry stashed in the pocket of my frilly apron buzzed, making me twitch, which in turn caused the bubbling fondue pot to spit a fleck of boiling oil into my ear. *"Thppft!"* I said brightly, biting my tongue.

Did I mention I had already been fired once this summer for swearing on the job?

Regaining my balance, I unshipped the platter of gleaming cubed steak, cubed pork, cubed chicken, and—our specialty— cubed sausage. Next I needed to get ice water and kiddie menus for Table 9. I snuck a peek at the Blackberry on my way back to the serving station.

```
J
listen I'm on my way to CA—
should get there tomorrow
sometime.  i need to know
where u are.  Gonna ship out
soon.  Need to pick u up before
i go.
D
```

I WANT YOU

Oh, man.

So now Jewel's poor brother was driving across America to pick me up, on the assumption I was Jewel. YIKES. I reread the message. Whoa: *Ship out?!?* I had positively, absolutely, for certain decided that I wasn't going to answer any more of Denny's messages, but that was before reading this. Angrily I thumbed a reply.

> **Denny! Ship out! Ur joining
> the army? R u crazy?!?!?**

84 I stuck the Blackberry back in my apron and gathered up supplies for the Fun Family at Table 9. I put the kiddie menus in front of three silent children who were all looking nervously at their mother, a lean woman in a tie-dyed shirt. She looked like a prison guard from Camp Groovy. I dug in my apron pocket for double helpings of the crayons that came with the Junior Mountaineers Menu. "Management only wants to give out two crayons per kid, but I like to encourage art in my section," I said with my best Friendly Waitress smile.

"We don't need to waste resources," Fun Mom said.

"You won't. Aren't," I said nervously. "We reuse them."

"These are some other kid's crayons?" said the biggest Fun Kid.

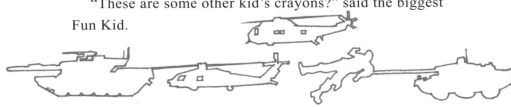

"There's only two colors," said Fun Kid #2. "Red and white."

"I think it's a theme," the dad said weakly. "Like the shield and cross on Daddy's Swiss Army"—he glanced guiltily at his wife—"tool."

"I want the red ones," said the littlest Fun Tot.

"I don't want some other kid's *germs*."

"This isn't tap water, is it?" Fun Mom said.

"It's distilled," I said.

The Blackberry buzzed again. "Whoops! There's a customer who needs me! I'll be right back to take your order."

I snuck another peek at the phone.

```
Probation ofc sed if i joined
up cops wd drop charges.
Stop changing the subject.
```

I felt myself shaking with anger. I could just imagine some probation officer thinking, "Ah, what the hell—let's just make this guy the Army's problem. If he gets his ass shot off, who's gonna give a damn?"

Let it go, Cathy, I told myself. I found my smile and stuck it back on. *Customer service is my passion,* I said to myself. *Customer service is my life.*

The fussy woman Nora had seated at Table 13 was forty-five or so, wearing the Official Uniform of the Bay Area's Fashionably Middle-Aged: tasteful pants and a Prada handbag, a champagne-colored silk blouse, and, for added excitement, one of those Artistic Wraps knitted from acid green yarn that looked as if a cat had barfed on it. Dyed hair, of course, from a bottle with a name like Burnt Sienna or Sun-Warmed Brick. "Can I have a Half-Caff Non-Fat Caramel Latte?" she said.

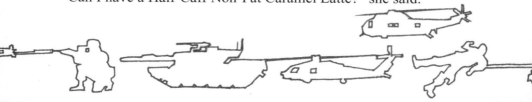

"Did I hear you tell that other table that management is stingy with crayons?" she added, taking a notebook out of her Prada handbag.

My Spidey-sense started tingling. "Oh, that's just something I do with kids."

"But that is what you said, isn't it? And you gave them extra crayons." A mechanical pencil had appeared between her fingers to hover over her notebook like a scorpion's tail.

"Half-caff non-fat caramel latte and a menu," I said brightly. "Coming up."

Next, over to the bar to pick up a bottle of St. Pauli Girl for Table 6. While the bartender fished it out of his cooler, I dragged out the Blackberry and thumbed a furious reply to Jewel's brother.

Denny. If yr heart says u have
to go, go. But they KILL people
over there. u want to get blown
up? u want to kill 13 yr old Iraqi
girls w hand grenades?

Table 6 was a young guy wearing a suit and a smirk. His lips were the color of earthworms. Vice-president of marketing for a tech start-up, if I had to guess, or possibly a mutual fund salesman. His smirk broadened as I put down his beer.

86.

"Say, the print on this menu is really small. I'm having trouble reading it." He pointed at one of the entrees. "What does that say?"

"I think…" I peered down where he was pointing, but he kept tilting the menu so it was hard to read. I leaned forward until I felt a draft blowing from my throat to my navel.

Looking down, I realized I could see all the way down my frilly shirt to my knees. I snapped upright, grabbing the collar of my AlpenBlouse. "Eyes to yourself, creep!"

Heads snapped around to look at me from all over the section. I felt my cheeks burning. Earthworm Lips sniggered into his bottle of St. Pauli Girl. Over at Table 13, Cat Barf's eyebrows rose and her mechanical pencil went scritching furiously across her notebook. I stalked back to the coffee station to get Cat Barf her order. Nobody had made any decaf espresso. Of course.

I returned to Table 13. "We're just making a fresh pot of decaf," I told Cat Barf with my most reassuring smile. "This will only take a second."

"Were you sending a text message a few minutes ago?"

"No!"

"Didn't I see you doing something with your thumbs?"

"Arthritis," I said. "It acts up on me if I don't keep them limber." I waggled my thumbs. "Runs in the family," I said. Cat Barf looked unconvinced.

The Blackberry buzzed. I pretended not to notice.

"What's that?" Cat Barf asked.

"What's what?"

Another buzz, followed by a gong. Not a text message. A phone call. "Whoops! Kitchen needs me!" I said. *Bzzzt-GONG.* I trotted back to the kitchen as fast—*Bzzt-GONG*—as my clogs would carry me.

As soon as I was through the swinging doors to the kitchen I grabbed the phone. It was Emma. "Yeah?" I said, wondering where I was going to find decaf beans to load into the espresso machine.

"Listen, Tsao is taking me to the opera tonight to meet some investors and we were hoping you could come along."

"Emma, I know he's been very generous, but didn't anyone ever tell you to look a gift horse in the mouth?"

"I thought that's what you weren't supposed to—"

I found the coffee beans. No decaf. I grabbed a handful of regular and ground those instead. "Whatever. My point is, middle-aged rich guys don't usually start unloading cash on young, uh…"

"Businesses," Emma said tartly. "Don't be paranoid."

I headed out of the kitchen, smiling brightly at Cat Barf's table, and loaded the new espresso into the machine as if this was a special grind of decaf just for her.

"Something else," Emma said. "I was looking more carefully at Parkinson's file on your dad. It doesn't have a phone number or a home address, but under 'contact' it does list a post office box."

"That's weird." I could feel Cat Barf's eyes boring into my back like a pair of thumbtacks as I poured a shot of espresso for her Half-Caff Non-Fat Caramel Latte. "Hey, Emma, you can't actually taste caffeine, can you?"

"No, I think it's odorless and tasteless, like the better class of poisons."

"No personal calls!" Nora the Hostess hissed, on her way to one of the twenty-three cigarette breaks she took every day.

"The PO box is at the main post office," Emma went on. "I've been there, it's just a big bank of metal boxes, but they aren't in a secured area or anything, so you don't have to have ID to get to them, you just have to show up … as long as you've got the key."

"Key!" I whispered. I had a vivid memory of my father's studio, as clear in my mind's eye as a still life painting. He didn't like having anything in his pockets when he painted, so he always left his wallet on the worktable and his key ring dangling from a thumbtack pushed into the top of his easel. "I bet I know exactly where that is."

"Brilliant!" Emma said.

Nora's long fingernail, a cherry-red dagger that would have looked right at home on Cruella DeVille, appeared over my shoulder and hit the Hang Up button on the Blackberry. "No personal calls," she wheezed. She coughed, hacked, and spat a tobacco-colored loogie into a coffee cup. "We gotta look professional."

Environmentally Correct Fondue (Hour of the Wholly Unionized Cows)

OK, Cathy: get your priorities straight.

It was extremely important for the rest of my life that I find out more about what had happened to my father, and the box at the post office was an excellent lead. It also felt very important that over the next few days I manage to convince Denny not to throw his life away by joining the army. But my chief goal over the next few minutes needed to be Not Getting Fired, because between all the orders and phone calls and texting I was feeling more and more like I was juggling chain saws, and someone had greased the handles on them. One conversation I did NOT want to have was the one where I explained to my mother that although we had agreed I would start paying a modest rent every month, I was going to have to back out, for

the second month out of two, because I had been fired. Again.

I bore down on my Waitress Kung Fu, and executed the next few minutes of my shift to perfection:

- Half-Caff Non-Fat Caramel Latte to Cat Barf Lady: check.
- Drink refills for the Mixed Meats: check.
- Order up for Worm Lips: check on that, and service with a scowl, no extra charge.

The Blackberry buzzed again, but this time I played it smart. I headed briskly into the women's washroom, walked into a stall, pulled the door shut and slid the lock over before taking out the Blackberry.

> Jesus, J. Since when did
> you start watching the news?

Hmm. Might be slipping out of character there. Better watch that. Funny: an hour ago I was totally resolved never to pretend to be Jewel again. Now it seemed desperately important that I make the lie work. Denny was willing to drive halfway across the country to pick up a good-for-nothing sister who was about as much fun as a hail storm on a nude beach. Victor wouldn't even return my email messages. Denny could get shipped to Iraq and die a thousand ways for no damn reason at all. Just because he was expendable. Victor couldn't die even if he tried.

"Expendable" wasn't a Jewel word, though. Had to be careful with that. With shaking thumbs I typed:

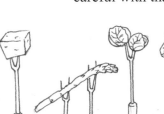**You r not nothing.**

**We need u. I
need u. Stay here.**

Then it was back to the Fun Family.

Warden Mom looked up, her face gaunt from a few too many Fun Runs for the Environment, frown lines deepening. "I'm a little disappointed with your menu."

"Disappointed?"

"We don't eat meat."

"Any of you?"

Fun Tot nodded glumly.

"What am I supposed to order, here?" Warden Mom said.

"Well, there's cheese fondue—"

"We're vegans."

"No dairy products allowed," the dad said apologetically.

"Or eggs," the oldest kid added.

"Or honey," her brother said.

Honey? I guess it qualified as exploiting the labor of unconsenting bugs.

"Did you happen to notice the name of the restaurant?" I asked, flexing my Perky Waitress smile.

"Obviously I assumed you would *specialize* in fondue," the mother said, "but not even a few vegan options? I have to say, I'm a little … disappointed."

Panic rose in my throat in a very familiar way. I was getting to be quite an expert at getting fired, and like an old sailor I could feel the winds shifting to just north of Unemployment, and picking up speed.

"No problem!" I burbled. "We have a *chocolate* fondue!"

Warden Mom's frown deepened. "For a main course?"

"Guaranteed meat-free and fun for the whole family!"

"But—"

"Our dessert fondues are made from chocolate hand picked by small worker-owned collectives in South America," I added quickly. "The collectives are modeled on our Free-Range Voluntary Milk Contribution Cheese Factories, which plow profits back into buying better feed for our wholly unionized cows."

"Chocolate?" said the Fun Tot.

"Chocolate," I said, locking eyes with each kid in turn and speaking very deliberately. "All. The chocolate. You. Can. Eat."

Warden Mom said, "I really don't think…" and then subsided as a low snarl rumbled through someone's throat. It might have been her husband.

Mom smiled weakly. "We'll have the Family Fun Pot, then," she said. "But if you could make that with brown sugar…?"

As I left the table I put my order pad in front of my face to hide my smile.

Later That Afternoon (Hour of the Deducted Dry Cleaning Bill)

It's a funny thing, isn't it, how Pride Goeth Before the Fall?

Here's what happened, exactly the way the Fondue! lawyer said I should explain it if anything actually went to trial. I was just coming out of the kitchen with a pot of melted chocolate for the Fun Family when the Mixed Meats stopped me and tried to ask a question. They were turning slowly red and there was a lot of mumbling, so I kept leaning closer and closer to

hear what they were saying. I finally figured out that they were asking where they could buy the Fondue! uniforms. I was trying to think of a tactful way of asking if they were interested in the leather shorts, such as Todd was wearing, or my own Peasant Blouse-and-Miniskirt ensemble. Then I heard Worm Lips bark out, "I wouldn't mind skiing them moguls!" just as I felt a draft on my butt.

I straightened up and whirled around to give him one of my witty put-downs, the kind that would leave a handprint tattooed on his smirking face, only to find that the spot I was whirling into was now filled with Cat Barf, the customer from Table 13, saying, "I can taste the caffeine! I can taste the caffeine!"

Even smacking into the lady from Table 13 wouldn't have been so bad, if her Artistic Wrap and Prada handbag hadn't been so very, very expensive, and the pot of melted chocolate on my serving tray so very, very tippy. So then suddenly we were both sitting down, and I was wearing an expression of extreme dismay, and she was wearing a Family Fun Chocolate Pot.

—which is when I found out another thing that the Management of Fondue! liked to do, which was

- Hire Secret Shoppers to evaluate the staff. Which explained all of Table 13's nosy questions and her furious note taking.

In case you ever wondered, throwing a pot of melted chocolate on a Secret Shopper is, indeed, enough to get you fired.

My Brother's Keeper (Hour of My Sister Under the Skin)

I turned in my AlpenBlouse and miniskirt and clogs. To add insult to injury, I had to borrow money from Nora the Chain-Smoking Hostess to get home. I had just trudged to the nearest BART station when the Blackberry buzzed again.

```
> You r not nothing.
> We need you. I need
> you.  Stay here.

Where's "here"?  In San Jose
tomorrow.  Need to know where
u r.  Put up or shut up, J.
```

Right. In all the excitement I had forgotten Jewel's brother was going to be arriving in northern California in a day. I had a brief fantasy of giving him my address and then leaving a note on the kitchen table explaining to him that I wasn't his sister and he had driven across the country for no reason. In the same note I would tell my mom I had been fired and was running away from home. They would bond over their mutual rage and disgust for me, after which my mother would adopt Denny and put him through medical school in exchange for him doing maintenance on our old Mercury Marquis. For my part, I would live in the Dumpster behind Shiny Simon's Drive-Thru Car Wash, on the theory that I could get a free shower there every morning.

Be honest now: who in her secret heart hasn't wanted to walk through a car wash on foot?

I allowed myself to live in this happy fantasy until the BART train pulled out of the station. Then it was time to consider more realistic alternatives.

THE
WALK AND
WASH

The idea of having Denny come and haul Jewel out of California was extremely attractive. Plus maybe between Jewel and me we could talk him out of the idea of joining the Army. On the other hand, I had no idea where Jewel was staying, and no way to find out.

Hang on. Wait. That wasn't quite true, was it?

I did know one thing about Jewel—I knew a phone number where I could reach her. I waited until the train was above ground and dialed my own number, the number of the cell phone she had stolen from me. Someone picked up. "Hello, Jewel?"

"Cathy! Great to hear from you!" she said brazenly.

"Look, I want my phone back."

"Hey, I traded fair and square. Really, the Blackberry's an upgrade. Haven't you sold it yet?"

"Sold it? No. I put it back in the mail to Chad," I said, realizing I really ought to do that right away.

"That's funny. Caller ID said this WAS Chad."

Oops. Busted. "Listen, I've been talking to Denny." Silence. The BART train clackity-clacked down the South Bay. A big airplane roared down low over the water on my left, coming in to land at the airport. "Denny as in your brother," I said.

"How in the hell—"

"That doesn't matter right now," I said. "What matters is that he'll be in town tomorrow. He's coming to pick you up."

"He can try," Jewel said.

"Also, he's joining the Army."

"He always says that."

"Well, this time his probation officer is telling him to."

Jewel swore. "If he wants to get his ass shot off, that's his business."

The train slowed, pulling into the station at San Bruno. "They don't get shot in the ass, Jewel. This isn't a cartoon. They get their legs blown off with land mines. They get kidnapped and beheaded and the guys who did it put the video up on the internet."

Silence.

"He's gonna be here tomorrow, Jewel."

"You have this idea about family," Jewel said. "You think there's some white picket fence waiting at home. Listen, the best thing I can do for Denny is to stay the hell away from him, OK? I have a thing going here that's gonna take care of him and Momma and everybody else."

"This I gotta hear," I said.

"I don't need your help, Cathy, and you aren't my friend. We are not buddies, and I ain't telling you what I'm doing or where I'm at."

"When Denny shows up, you need to talk to him." No response. The train pulled forward, heading east. "Jewel. I could have you arrested. I don't want to do that, but I need you to talk to your brother. Also, I want my damn phone back."

"I sort of wondered why you hadn't had it disconnected."

"I wanted to be able to reach you." This was a lie, but it sounded better than *I'm barely organized enough to get my underwear on the right side of my clothes.* "But if you won't talk to Denny, I'll cut off the service."

"No, wait," Jewel said quickly. "Listen, I'm sorry I took your phone. That was wrong. But things are going really good for me now. I met this guy, he's really sweet and he's loaded, too."

I cringed. Someone said something to Jewel in the background. "Hang on a sec," she said. She must have covered

96.

the receiver with her hand. I heard a muffled conversation between her and some guy, but I couldn't make out any of the words until she came back on the line. "Okay, how about we get together tomorrow and I'll give you your phone back?"

That seemed suspiciously easy, but after a little dickering we agreed to meet at noon the following day at the food court in the mall near my house. As soon as I hung up, I sent a text message back to Denny with my address. As for how exactly I would get the two of them together, well, I would blow up that bridge when I came to it.

Now all I had left to do was tell my mom I had been fired. I settled back in my seat on the train. I had nothing to do for the next quarter hour except let the dread build.

You Made Him So Proud

"Fired? Again?" my mom said. It was five o'clock, almost time for her to go to work. She was standing in front of the bathroom mirror brushing her hair in short, angry strokes. "I had to call in favors to get you that job," she said.

"I know."

"Two days." She pulled her hair back and twisted it into a tight, professional ponytail. A lot of women get plumper in middle age, but my mom was going the other way. She didn't eat much and she ate without pleasure, as if resenting the time it took. "You lasted two days."

"Yeah." I felt stupid standing in the bathroom doorway so I walked into the kitchen and looked in the freezer to see if we had any frozen pizzas left I could make for dinner. My cheeks were burning. It was easier not to face her. "It was actually kind of funny what happened," I said. "There was this—"

"Kind of funny?" My mother left the bathroom and came into the kitchen. I could feel her eyes on my back. "Is this a joke to you, Cathy?"

"No, it's not a—"

"Do you think the real world is like high school? You think you can just not give a damn and it doesn't matter?"

"I tried, Mom! It was just bad luck. There was this—"

"And here come the excuses," she said. The cold air from the freezer stung my face. "Well? Let's hear 'em, kiddo."

"Never mind."

"Come on, Cathy. I love a good excuse."

I turned around. "No excuse," I said. "I just suck that much."

My mom turned her back on me, digging her sensible nurse shoes out of the closet. "How's that website coming? The one you were going to make to sell your art. Done anything on that yet?" I didn't say anything. "You used to work so hard on your drawings. You would come rushing back from school with a notebook full of pictures and run up to the studio. Because you always wanted to impress your father," she said. "You always wanted to make him proud."

"You could try being proud of me, too," I said, my voice tight.

"You could try giving me a reason." Mom straightened up and grabbed her purse. "Your part of the rent is due in five days," she said, getting out her car keys. "Tell me if you aren't going to have it. I'd like a little warning."

I headed for my room.

"I thought you were going to get some dinner," Mom said. Her voice hard.

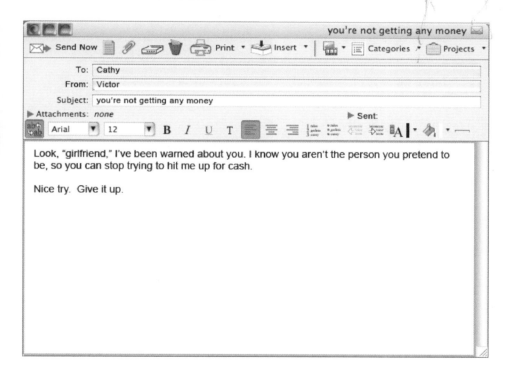

"I'm not hungry," I shouted.

"Good," she said. "Food isn't cheap."

Mail from Victor (Hour of the Ex-Girlfriend)

I stalked into my bedroom and slammed the door behind me. Out of pure reflex I checked my inbox and finally there was an email from Victor.

---

you're not getting any money ✉

Send Now | Print ▾ | Insert ▾ | Categories ▾ | Projects ▾

To: Cathy
From: Victor
Subject: you're not getting any money
Attachments: *none* ▶ Sent:

Arial | 12 | **B** *I* U T

Look, "girlfriend," I've been warned about you. I know you aren't the person you pretend to be, so you can stop trying to hit me up for cash.

Nice try. Give it up.

He hadn't even bothered to put his name at the bottom.

The door to my bedroom opened. "*Knock*, damn it!" I shouted.

"I'm going to work," Mom said. "I forgot to tell you before, your friend dropped by."

"What friend?" I said, deleting Victor's email. My hand

was shaking as I moved the mouse. I couldn't bear the idea that she would see that message.

"From your Business of Art camp," my mother said. "Jewel."

That got my attention. *"What?* Jewel was *here?"*

"Don't worry, I wasn't *embarrassing*," my mother said bitterly. "I made her feel right at home."

Thief (Hour of the Missing Scarf)

So on top of everything else, while I was raiding Dr. Parkinson's office, Jewel had actually come by my house and hung out with my mother! I did a furious inventory of my room. As I expected, she had helped herself to some of my stuff, specifically:

- Various clothes, especially shirts and underwear
- Several drawings
- Pretty much all of my makeup except what I'd been carrying in my purse
- A white silk scarf, World War I aviator style, that Victor had given me

I didn't cry until I realized the scarf was missing.

I had met this girl on a Greyhound bus, for God's sake. Now she had my phone. She had my clothes. She had the last present Victor had given me. From the moment I met her, it was as if he had forgotten about me. I opened the trash folder and reread his email, in case I had misunderstood the tone, but the second time through it was just as curt and contemptuous.

On top of all that, Jewel had poisoned my head with the idea that my dad might still be alive somewhere, having walked out on me like all the men in her life had walked out on her. After all, if Parkinson was really a friend of my dad's, the contact information in my father's file should have listed our phone number and address. I wanted to be mystified by that, but I could hear Jewel whispering that there was no mystery here at all. *Don't you get it, sugar? Your daddy didn't give him a home phone number because they were never friends. Parkinson was strictly a business partner, and anything he had for your dad was something you and your momma were never, ever supposed to see.*

I squeezed my eyes shut and tried to get her voice out of my head. It wasn't as if I could blame everything on her. The Fondue! job I had lost on my own … but partly because I had been so bloody distracted by the Blackberry and the messages from her brother. Right?

I got out my sketchbook and stared at the drawings I had done of Jewel. Those pickpocket eyes.

From the moment we met, our destinies had gotten tangled up. Day by day she was stealing more and more of my life, and day by day, I was falling more and more helplessly into hers.

Next Day at the Food Court (Hour of the Evil Twin)

The local mall was three stories tall, with an atrium at one end that arched up like a Cathedral of Commerce. Escalators like beams and buttresses crossed the tall space, and every floor was ringed by store window mannequins who stood posed like saints nested in their niches. At the bottom of this vaulted space was the food court. I was expecting something of a showdown with Jewel and I had dressed accordingly: fitted Western-style vest over ripped T-shirt, skinny jeans and shoes with enough heel to announce my presence with authority, but not so much I couldn't run in them if I had to. Or kick people, even.

Jewel showed up twenty minutes late. She had dyed her hair dark brown, like mine, and done her eye makeup the way I did mine as well. She was wearing Victor's white silk scarf over one of my shirts. She was also walking on a man's arm. It was Tsao. Jewel gave me a little wave. "Cathy! I think you know my date?"

"Hello, Cathy," Tsao said. He held out his hand, and I shook it. Time slowed.

Jewel was drenched in perfume, a powerful scent with the fragrance of peaches that almost stopped my breath when she leaned in and gave me a hug. Her newly colored hair whispered around my shoulders. "Don't look so shocked," Jewel laughed. "Didn't I tell you I'd met a guy who could help me out?"

My brain slowly started to get unstuck. "My diary," I said. "You took it. You found his business card."

"I keep trying to talk to you," Tsao said. "You have been avoiding me."

"That's my scarf," I said.

Jewel ran her hand down the smooth white silk. "It's Victor's scarf. I'm just borrowing it for a few years."

"Victor! How the hell do you know…" And then, finally, the light dawned. "You had my cell phone," I whispered. "You called Victor."

"I never did," Jewel said.

My mind was racing. "That's right, he would have recognized your voice … but you could text him," I said. "Caller ID would say it was my phone! Any message you sent him, he would think was from me. That's what you did, too. You told him not to trust anything coming from my email account."

"Identity theft," Jewel said. "You hear about it all the time these days."

And *that* was why Victor hadn't returned my first email, and sent back such a crushing reply to the second. Fury pounded through me as I looked at Jewel, wearing my clothes and my scarf, her hair dyed to match mine. "You two-faced, lying creep—you've been pretending to be me!"

"How did you know my brother's name?" Jewel said. Quick as a snake.

My heartbeat smashed in my chest, *bang, bang, bang.*

"You and me," Jewel drawled, "separated at birth, that's what I think."

Vertigo (Hour of Death and Desire)

Tsao said, "I would like to talk to Cathy alone."

"I don't want to miss all the fun," Jewel pouted. She held up a little perfume bottle. "You should try this stuff," she said, squirting me with the peach-scented perfume. "It's super expensive."

Tsao adjusted his diamond cufflinks. When he looked up at Jewel, his eyes were empty. As if a human life—her life—was a cigarette butt on the sidewalk: something to step over, or grind out. "Go eat," he said.

"Can I at least have some money to get—"

"You've been paid."

"At least make her give me my phone back," I said. "God knows I—"

"Later," Tsao barked. Once again I was surprised, as I had been when he shouted at Mr. Cheung in Emma's apartment. It was so unlike Tsao to give way to these sudden bursts of temper. He collected himself and produced his usual suave smile. "If you could just spare me a moment?" He dropped his hand to the small of my back and with the lightest possible touch began to steer me away from the food court.

Time slowed again. The sounds of the mall went thin and distant, as if heard through a phone. I could feel each of Tsao's fingertips through my shirt, spots of heat that seemed to spread out across my skin. "Where are we going?" I managed to say. "I want to stay in a public place."

Tsao guided me to the escalators and we stepped on. "You should stop acting as if I were your enemy. Nothing could be further from the truth." Down in the food court, Jewel watched us ascend. "You are in trouble, Cathy. You have no money and no prospects of getting any. You are caught in a war between immortals and you have powerful enemies. You need a protector."

"What enemies?"

"Ancestor Lu, for one. His daughter, Jun, for another.

She's afraid Victor might come back to you," Tsao said, with a shrug. "I suppose she's worried that even after she marries Victor he might still harbor inappropriate feelings for you."

My heart dropped like an elevator with the cable cut, and smashed to the bottom of my chest. "After she marries Victor?"

"I've been trying to tell you about their engagement for days," Tsao said. "Didn't you receive any of my messages?"

I deleted them unread, I didn't say.

We stepped off the escalator on the third floor and walked slowly past a sports bar, a shoe store, a Sunglass Shed and a video game store. I forced myself to remember the day Victor had snuck away from Lu's lab and kissed me in the Burger Barn. Get me fired, yeah, that he might do. But leave me for Jun two weeks later? "You're lying," I said.

Tsao put his elegantly manicured hands on the glass half-wall that ringed the atrium. "I like high places. The view is always … clarifying. Cathy, Victor's whole life has been walking out on women before they discover him, or leave him, or die. Think what it would mean to finally find a woman *with whom he could share eternity.*"

It's a lie, it's a lie, it's a lie, I told myself. But it wasn't, not that part. Victor had always been haunted by his immortality. He had abandoned every family he'd ever made, every home he'd ever found. Jun was smart, beautiful, passionate, and above all, she was like him. She was the one woman he could share everything with—forever.

Up here on the third floor the stores were almost empty. Noise rose up from the food court below, a confused babble. Tsao leaned on the atrium rail next to me, elegant in Armani, tainted just a little with the scent of Jewel's peach perfume.

"You could use a friend," he said gently.

"And you're volunteering." A sparrow had wandered into the mall through some open door and now found itself trapped. It flicked up through the atrium toward us, trying to find a way back into the open air. "Would you show me around, treat me nice, buy me things?" I asked. "Like Jewel?"

Tsao grimaced. "She is nothing to me."

"I know that. Does she?" As I watched, the sparrow tried one of the skylights and banged awkwardly off the glass.

Tsao ignored me. "Wouldn't you like to stop worrying about money, stop working these terrible jobs that are so very much beneath you? Or did you enjoy your time at the Burger Barn?"

He had me there.

"Cathy, I've been a rich man for a very long time. An amount of money I wouldn't even notice would mean freedom for you," he said gently. "Freedom to paint and draw and follow your real passion. Freedom to live the life you deserve."

He made it sound very lovely, but I was too much my mother's daughter to believe in a free lunch. "In junior high we learned a bad word for girls who take money for nothing."

"Fine," he said impatiently. "Then consider yourself the graphic designer for DoubleTalk Wireless."

"That would be for Emma to decide," I said. "And honestly, I do sketches and doodles. A graphic treatment for a serious business—Emma deserves a professional to do that."

Tsao laughed. "DoubleTalk is not a serious business, Cathy. It exists because I thought it would please you." He touched my hand very lightly and once again heat seeped into my skin from his fingertips. "A present from me to you is all that company ever was."

106.

I pulled my hand away. "But … haven't you been taking Emma to meet investors? Like at the symphony the other night?"

"I have been creating chances to be with *you*." The hand that had touched mine curled into a fist. "Which, I might add, you have been avoiding to the point of rudeness."

Oh, man, this was going from bad to worse. "Do you realize that Emma's dad thinks you're going to marry her?"

"Oh, so you noticed that, did you?" Tsao laughed. "A peculiar form of virgin sacrifice still practiced in these modern times," he said contemptuously. "You'd be amazed how many earnest young daughters of greedy businessmen are thrown in my path, my dear. It's positively feudal. God knows I could have bedded your friend by now, if I had a taste for … discount merchandise."

I felt physically sick with rage and dismay. "Do you even give a damn about Emma?"

"Greed bores me," Tsao said. "That's one of the things I love about you, Cathy. Money has no power over your imagination." Once again he dropped his hand to the small of my back. I tried to twist away, but he was strong, far stronger than he seemed, and somehow I couldn't move. I was pinned against the glass wall, with the brass rail pressing into my stomach. Tsao's head bent toward mine until his skin touched my hair and I could feel his breath on my neck. "Cathy, I need you. I need you like a falcon needs the wind."

"Let me go!"

Tsao's hand pressed harder, flattening against my back. I tipped forward, bending over the atrium rail until my heels came off the ground. I was leaning far out over the rail. It was a long way down to the marble floor. I imagined the

107.

drop, tumbling and screaming, the sick plunge and my heart hammering in my chest, and then the sudden obliterating smack as I hit the food court floor, ribs splintering, skull cracked open like an egg.

"Please," I whispered. "You're scaring me."

"Why do you make me so angry?" Tsao whispered. "I could be such a good friend, Cathy." I bucked back against his hand, trying desperately to stop my slow slide over the atrium rail, but all that did was put me more off balance and I slid a little further out into space.

Tsao's cultured Oxford voice was quiet, almost hypnotic. "Do you want to see Emma's business thrive? I can make her a millionaire, if that's what you want. Or she and her unspeakable father can be living in a Dumpster in three days' time. Your choice, Cathy." He tipped me forward another inch so even my toes came off the floor and I was seconds from sliding over the rail and plunging to the marble floor below.

"This isn't love," I gasped.

"This is *exactly* what love is," Tsao hissed. "I have gone hundreds of years without wanting anything, Cathy. Centuries of dust in my veins, until nothing is left but the terrible aching desire to desire." He pushed harder still and I squirmed as my body tipped further over the railing. "Now I want again, and what I want is you. I will have you, willing or not, living or dead."

"I'll scream," I said.

"Yes," he said. "I know."

Lucky Fortune for You

"Hey!" said a sharp voice. "Mr. Tsao!"

Tsao spun around, startled, and gave me an accidental push. I pitched forward into space—

And then a big black hand grabbed my arm and jerked me back. It was Auntie Joe, massive in polyester pants that seemed to magnify her enormous rump and a T-shirt with two gigantic fried eggs on the front emphasizing her other assets. She was carrying a 20-ounce can of beer and a sardonic expression. "Wow! Imagine meeting you guys here! That's a hell of a coincidence. You got to be careful with these," she told Tsao, jerking a thumb at me. "They break easy."

I twisted and dropped so I had my back to the glass wall as I crouched between the two immortals. Tsao blinked and shook his head like a man waking from a dream. "This isn't like me," he whispered. "Something is wrong. I haven't felt this way in a thousand years. I haven't felt this way since…" He looked down at me, ashen-faced.

"Since before you murdered your first love," I said.

"Since before I became what I am." His expression slowly hardened. "What have you done to me?"

Auntie Joe laid a meaty hand on Tsao's shoulder. "Sugar, I don't think Cathy is the source of your problems."

There was a whiff of peach-scented perfume in the air. I turned and saw Jewel stepping off the escalator. "Too long," she pouted. "I'm bored." Jewel hooked one hand possessively on Tsao's arm. "Do you like my perfume?" she said, fixing Auntie Joe with her big fake Texas smile. "Try it out!" And she squirted a misty cloud of the stuff that sparkled like dew drops in Auntie Joe's hair and settled into her beer.

"Hey now," the fortune-teller said, peering down into the can. "That's just wrong."

"Take your hands off me," Tsao said coldly to Auntie Joe. "As for you, Cathy, you've made your choice. Bed my son, if you ever see him again. But don't come whining to me when he throws you away. You'll never get another offer like mine."

"Go to hell," I said. "Listen, Jewel, you don't matter to him. He's just going to use you up and throw you away." I caught a flicker of uncertainty in her eyes. "Come back with me," I said. "Go home with your brother. You don't have to stay with this creep."

"Yes," Tsao said curtly, putting his hand on her arm. "She does."

Jewel's shoulders sagged. She closed her eyes and for one moment I thought I had convinced her, but when she opened them again they were bright and hard. "I don't need charity from *you*," she said. "I got big things working. I got a plan."

*

"Wow," I said to Auntie Joe, after Tsao and Jewel had gone. "Talk about showing up in the nick of time!"

Auntie Joe grinned. "Like I said before, what about the words 'sees the future' don't you understand?"

"Okay, I get that. But I still don't see … I mean, why are you looking out for me?"

"Oh, I been paid. There's a certain interested party as asked me to keep an eye on you," Auntie Joe said with a sly smile. The slyness slowly faded, and then the smile, too. "And you and me … let's just say this meeting means as much to me as it does to you," she said cryptically.

"I don't understand."

"I know." The trapped sparrow took off from a potted plant outside the sports bar and did another turn around the skylights, vainly looking for a way out. Auntie Joe and I watched it flit and dart through the echoing air until it banged into the glass window of the video game store and staggered back to perch on the edge of a trash can. "Just cuz Auntie Joe can see the future, that don't mean she can change it," the big woman said. She took another long pull on her can of beer. "I do win a lot of money at the dog track, though."

It was the last thing I would ever hear her say.

112.

Me llena de satisfacción poder informar a Vuestras Altezas que las preparaciones para nuestra gloriosa misión a las islas norteñas andan bien. Los taínos hablan continuamente de las generosas riquezas que se encuentran al norte, y también de maravillas aún más increíbles que el oro y las perlas.

Ayer arribó de Grenada el Guía de quién tuvieron a bien escribirme. Es sano y joven a pesar de su edad. De hecho, uno de los marineros viejos me dijo que el hombre le daba cuenta de un hombre el cual servía bajo las órdenes de Colón hace más de quince años, aunque no puede creer que sea la misma persona. De acuerdo con vuestras órdenes, induje a uno de mis soldados a provocarle en la taberna la noche pasada, y a día de hoy la herida que hace unas horas sangraba profusamente se ha convertido en nada mas que una blanca cicatriz. Yo le interrogué sobre las aguas curativas de las cuales dice que recibió su vitalidad, y su historia concuerda con varias leyendas aquí contadas que tratan de una fuente o río que transforma a viejos en fuertes mozos. Espero que pueda ayudarnos a navegar el mar desconocido y que nos sirva como explorador invencible contra la violencia de aquellos nativos que pudiésemos encontrar.

Que Vuestras Altezas me honoren con oraciones mientras prepare viajar por la gloria de Dios y de España y para aumentar la riqueza y la larga vida del reino.

Juan Ponce de León

1348. I was standing in St. Mark's Square, middle of Venice. Dead smack in the middle of the Black Death. Window opens up on the third story of a building across the
canal and someone slides a body out. The exact moment it hit the water, BAM, there
I was in this shopping mall. No words for it, of course. No words for "neon" and
"Styrofoam" and "soda fountain." No way to make sense of this mom stuffing french
fries into a kid with a Tickle Me Elmo hanging from her hand. I spent the next 650
years thinking, "What in the name of God Almighty was that?"

Other images.... Sitting down for tea with Ancestor Lu in the coffeehouse outside
the Sears, I can see that. Some funky herbal tea he's brought with him, smells like
peaches with a nasty aftertaste of antifreeze.

Another burst of static and I get Don Miguel's girl, in over her head as usual. You
can say I should never have agreed to look after her, but I knew I'd say yes to him
500 years before he asked, so there didn't seem any point in complaining.

Then, this part's always the same, I'm in a cubicle in some lonesome bathroom at the
bottom of the mall and I hear a door open. Under the door of my stall I can see a
pair of nice mens shoes walking toward me. Click clack, click clack.

At the end, it's harder to see. White. White tile floor, I guess, but something
else, too. White paper towels? White noise hissing in my ear. Not sure what the
whiteness is but it's cold and it feels so hard to breathe. Seems like I've spent a
thousand years wondering about that whiteness, but the picture's all broke up and I
can't make it out.

White nurse's uniform? White side of an ambulance?

I tell myself it doesn't matter. I tell myself it's time and past time for me. I
tell myself I've been ready since I woke up on the white sand of Egypt. But I can't
stop thinking about it, about what's going to happen to me. Refrigerator white?
Gauze white? Cotton bandage, maybe?

                                                                          ...Snowy

Good Lord, I don't want to have to be brave. Sweet Lord, give me the strength to en-
dure and the peace to accept.

IAN AYTON
NOTARY
PUBLIC
NOTARY
SEAL
CITY OF ST. LOUIS
STATE OF MISSOURI

BEING THE LAST WILL AND TESTAMENT OF AUNTIE JOE DUPREE, LATE OF ST. LOUIS, MISSOURI

I, Amunet Xanthippe Clio Marie Josephine "Auntie Joe" Dupree, being of ridiculously sound body and a mind no more scuffed up than usual, have a few last things to get out of my house and off my chest.

A good long time ago, a certain Queen of the Fourth Dynasty kicked the bucket. They scooped out all her organs and wrapped her up in over-priced sheets, and believe me, those shenanigans didn't make any more sense back in those days. Pharaoh's guards hustled us serving girls down into the pyramid too, as per her instructions. It was dark down there, and we were scared, and then they cut our throats and left us in the sand alongside the old hag so she could have folks to boss around and wash her nasty old feet in the afterworld, too.

Well, to my surprise I woke up a lot less dead than I expected and with my throat all unslit. I grabbed enough treasure out of the biddy's tomb to stay tolerably well off for the next thousand years or so and lit out for the territories. I also grabbed

TWO CANOPIC JARS, containing one (1) brain and two (2) eyeballs, respectively, which I leave to Scraps, my next-door neighbor's dog. To that certain Queen, all I have to say is, "How do you like them apples, Sweet Cheeks? C'mon, now, Scraps! Yum yum!"

To my godson, Jeremy Pine, who thinks he's all that, I leave RICHARD THE LIONHEART'S **CHAMBER POT**, as a reminder that no matter how much you think you are the bomb, you got to do the same thing when you get up in the morning as everybody else.

To the Boys and Girls Club of St. Louis I leave ONE (1) SET OF WOODEN TEETH BELONGING **TO GEORGE WASHINGTON.** Listen up, kids. Take it from Auntie Joe—the only thing I can guarantee about your future is that sixty years from now you will wish you had taken better care of your teeth.

THE REST OF MY WORLDLY GOODS AND POSSESSIONS I leave to the ladies of the Monday Morning Bingo Club. You're going to sell the contents of the house to the Smithsonian for 4.15 million bucks 'round about next fall. Live it up, girls.

As for the end...

You know how it is, you're driving and you start losing a station on the car radio, like it's steady blues, say, and then you get near the edge of broadcast range and the signal starts breaking up. Now the blues are coming in waves, but sometimes, in the trough of a wave, you get a sudden fragment of something else: country music out of Kansas, or rap thumping in from Ohio. Just a crackle of it and then it's gone. That's what the future is like. A distant signal, little pops and crackles of it between the waves of the present.

And at the end...? Signal breaks up and it's hard to understand, even for Auntie Joe. Food court of a shopping mall, that's one part. First time I saw that, it was

Fondue! Fantastic!
Merit Program

Employee Welcome!

Welcome to the Fondue! fun and dynamic Fondue! Fondue! is a family and entertainment Concept where Food is Fun. As an Employee, you are a member of the Concept team and part of the entertainment!

As a member of the Fondue! Team and exciting job that could become a career! But whether you are with us for a summer job or a lifetime, there are some basic positions you'll have to learn.

Fondue! Fantastic! Merit Points

Each store participates in the Fondue! Fantastic! program. As you, Fantastic! Earn Fantastic! Merit Points by accumulating Merit Points to customer components by presenting merit you are hired, and high scores in the waitstaff turning Leader to Fondue! Excellence! Tests.

- 10 pts. for customer Merit Points
- Fondue! Excellent card
- 10 pts. for a score of 99% or better on the test
- Leader to Fondue! Excellence! Tests
- 100 pts. for each person you recommend who is hired or further
- 10 pts. for Employee of the Month
- 100 pts. for Regional Employee of the Month

When you have accumulated enough Fondue! points, peruse the Fondue! Fantastic! Merit Catalogue. For 500 pts. choose the Fondue! pts. or claim the pts to earning set for 75,000 pts. earn them the trip to Switzerland! to enjoy classic fondue in authentic Swiss setting and spend the fun at the Cooking School to truly learn the secrets of fondue.

I seek my to open our an all rights to own behave and educate to person.

Uniforms

Fondue! employees must always be in full uniform. Two uniforms will be assigned to you, so you can launder one while wearing the other. You must be clean and neat.

Women's Uniforms

- Fondue! Nametag
- Alpine-style dirndl and Heidi-style torque
- Fondue! Swiss Apron™ with pockets for waitstaff order pad, change and pen. Do not carry personal items in the Fondue! Swiss Apron™ pockets. Weapons are not allowed in the restaurant.
- Clogs
- Hair must be pulled back during meal service at all times. No jewelry or earrings except small posts that meet approved Fondue! Fantastic! Merit Award jewelry
- All female employees must wear underpants. No thongs. THIS MEANS YOU.

Men's Uniforms

- Fondue! Nametag
- Alpine beige shirt and shwarm felt cap

- Fondue! Swiss Lederhosen™ with Fondue! Swiss Lederhosen™ pocket system for waitstaff order pad, change and pen. Do not carry personal items in the Fondue! Swiss Lederhosen™ pockets. Weapons are not allowed in the restaurant.
- Swiss buck buckle shoes
- Long hair must be pulled back, short hair is strongly encouraged. No earrings except small posts. No jewelry except Fondue! Fantastic! Merit prize. NO Swiss tattoos.

Fondue! Swiss Apron™ and Fondue! Swiss Lederhosen™ are available for purchase by staff or customers. These popular items are practical and fun!

sexy clogs (!)

Loser

XXXXXXXXXXXX

Ladder to Fondue! Excellence Tests!

Employees must take the Ladder to Fondue! Excellence Tests. These tests cover the menu, the policies in the employee manual, and the history of Swiss fondue starting with its invention in Swiss castles during ancient times. As you complete each rung on the ladder, you can add a crossed Fondue! forks emblem to your apron or cap. Once you have climbed to the top of the ladder, your name will be added to the Ladder to Fondue! Excellence Plaque at your restaurant site, proudly proclaiming your Excellence in all matters Fondue!

Great moments in the history of Fondue!

775: Charlemagne calls a dish of melted cheese fondue (French for melted), and declares it the National Dish of Switzerland and an honorary dish of the Holy Roman Empire.

1798: Presented with a meal of fondue (sliced chicken and hot oil with cognac, invented in his honor) Napoleon organizes a meeting of the leading Swiss politicians and ends the invasion of Switzerland by Austria and France.

1967: Pitchfork fondue, in which 8-ounce steaks are deep-fried in hot oil, is invented in Pindale, Wyoming.

certainly supports the majority view. Still, the alternate explanation is strong enough to merit continued study.

12. "...the interesting case of Miguel Allende...": A pair of recently discovered documents relate the mysterious and intriguing tale of Miguel Allende, a sixteenth century Spaniard and reluctant explorer. Strangely, both documents were discovered in the vaults of an Irish monastery.

The first of these documents is a transcript of Inquisition hearings in the city of Granada. The transcript is dated 1513 but appears to document proceedings that took place several months prior:

We, the Inquisition against depraved heresy and apostasy in the city of Granada. In the year of our Lord 1513, the twenty-ninth of May.

After receiving the testimony of a parishioner, we called Miguel Allende of Granada under suspicion of having practiced witchcraft in order to present an appearance of unnatural youth.

Therefore we called the man and questioned him. Over the course of several days, he denied that his youth was perverse and would only profess his faith in the cross. Weary of his pretense, we employed more persuasive means of interrogation. After several hours on the rack, having many broken bones, still he insisted upon his innocence. At length we brought in his daughter, a girl of sixteen. We questioned her extensively in his presence, and as we were heating the tongs in the fire, Allende finally confessed to having bathed in miraculous waters in the New World, waters which gave eternal youth and vigor. Very impressed by his ability to heal, we tested him by means of burning, drowning, and whipping, including "la garrucha." [*Also known as "manacuerda"; a form of torture in which the body of the accused was tied with rope and stretched on a rack. -Ed.*] That which follows is a complete account of his testimony under oath.

How old are you?

I am forty-three years old.

And so you have appeared for twenty years, and even your severest wounds heal before the following day. Have you achieved this through witchcraft or the dark arts?

I am a faithful Christian. I have never practiced either witchcraft or the dark arts.

Explain.

I sailed under Christopher Columbus to the New World nineteen years ago. During one of our expeditions, I became lost and was

captured by the natives. I learned some of their language, and they told me of a river that gives eternal youth to whatever person bathes in its waters. I asked them to take me to this place. After a long journey, they took me to the healing waters. During this time, I preached the Gospel to the natives, exhorting them to abandon their heretical ways and humble themselves before the Cross. I tried to teach them to pray, and clothe themselves as Christians, but they would not listen to me.

After many days of travel, we found the river, which was wide and calm. They took me to a place like a fountain. I bathed there and felt a deep peace. While I was bathing, the Holy Virgin Mary appeared and blessed me, and told me to return to Spain and care for my young daughter, and not to tell anyone about the waters.

Where is the river?

We traveled to the north many days, farther north than any place visited by Columbus. After, when I asked the Spaniards if they had found this place, they told me they had not seen it. I remember well the way to this place. If you would grant me a pen, I could draw a map right now, so that an explorer could find these waters.

Do you abjure all heresy and testify, that you have not practiced witchcraft and that you have had nothing to do with heretics?

I, Miguel Allende, swear to God and to you the bishops, to be a faithful and good Christian. I abjure all heresy. I swear that I have never practiced either witchcraft or the dark arts in any way. I swear that I have nothing to do with heretics. I swear to follow, uphold, and defend the Catholic faith that is taught and observed by the Catholic Church.

Having received this oath, the Archbishop absolved him, if he had simply and honestly testified the truth, and if he would return to the New World under the supervision of a missionary to guide an explorer to the fountain of youth so that others might benefit from these healing waters.

Then he pleaded with the Archbishop to allow him to draw a detailed map of the way to the fountain instead of traveling to San Juan Bautista [*modern Puerto Rico -Ed.*], saying that he had sworn to care for his daughter. The Archbishop ordered him to leave the following day, and promised that he himself would care for Miguel Allende's daughter and protect her until he returned with a jar of the miraculous water. In this way Allende could fulfill the instructions given by the Virgin Maria, because the Archbishop would care for his daughter. Ponce de Leon's mission failed and Allende was believed lost, but

Journal of Arch. Research - Vol. VII, Issue 12

55

ENDNOTES

parishioners reported that three years after leaving Granada he returned in disguise. Finding that his daughter had died in childbirth while under the Archbishop's care, he was said to have gone mad with grief, and no one has seen him since.

Made in the presence of the Archbishop of Granada by me, Juan Diego de Rivera, notary to my Lord the Archbishop.

The second record of Allende's travels in the New World is a letter penned by Ponce de Leon himself describing Allende's arrival. In the letter, de Leon says:

Ayer arrivó de Grenada el Guía de quién me escribisteis... uno de los marineros viejos me dijo que el hombre le daba cuenta de un hombre quien servía bajo Colón hace más de quince años, aunque no puede creer que es la misma persona. De acuerdo con vuestras órdenes, instruyé a uno de mis soldados a provocarle en la taberna la noche pasada, y hoy día la herida que hace unas horas sangraba libremente ya se ha puesto nada más que un cicatriz blanquito.

Yesterday the Guide about whom you wrote to me arrived from Granada... one of the old sailors told me that the man reminded him of a man who served under Columbus over 15 years ago, although he can't believe it is the same person. In keeping with your orders, I instructed one of my soldiers to provoke him in the tavern last night, and today the wound which several hours ago was bleeding freely has become nothing more than a small, white scar.

This pair of documents leads to the enticing notion that Ponce de Leon's doomed search for the mythical "Fountain of Youth" was in fact precipitated by an elaborate lie born of one man's desperate attempt to save himself and his daughter from the Inquisition. Occasional mentions of Allende in the journals of one of Ponce de Leon's men corroborates Allende's existence, if not the specifics of his tale.

Probationer's Name:			
Julia Marie "Jewel" Renfrew			Juvenile Case No: 58
Offense(s):		Probation Officer:	
Theft, Credit Card Abuse Evading Arrest		Luciana Mataka	
		Previous Offense(s): Simple Assault, Drug Offenses, Unlawful use of Motor Vehicle	

Probationer has been placed on Probation under the supervision of the probation officer named above. Probationer shall:

1. Attend school without unexcused absence or tardy.
2. Attend court hearings and probation meetings in a timely and respectful manner.
3. Not violate any criminal law of any unit of government.
4. Not leave the state without the consent of this court.
5. Make a truthful report to the probation officer _weekly_
6. Notify the probation officer immediately of any change of address, school, employment or phone number.
7. Not purchase or possess a firearm.
8. Not have contact with any person on probation, house arrest, or parole.
9. Comply with all Court orders, including but not limited to the following special terms of probation:

☐ Probationer poses a threat to the physical safety of 1 or more persons named here:

☒ Additions or amendments to these terms:

Exception to term 8 - probationer may have contact with step-father who is on parole in good standing. (LM)

Failure to comply with this order may result in a revocation of probation and incarceration in a juvenile detention facility.

Julia M Renfrew
Probationer

[signature]
Parent/Legal Guardian

Luciana Mataka
Probation Officer

Parent/Legal Guardian

Calling Victor (Hour of the Delayed Panic Attack)

During the time Tsao had been slowly pushing me over the atrium rail, a combination of fury and blind need to live had kept me from falling apart, but as I walked out of the mall five minutes later the full-bore panic arrived. My knees turned to jelly. I collapsed onto a bus stop bench and gripped the edge of it like a drowning woman grabbing a life preserver. My hands were shaking so badly I couldn't dial Victor's number on the Blackberry the first few times I tried, but finally the call went through.

No answer, of course. I waited for the beep. "Listen, jerk, I assume you can remember far enough back to recognize this is Cathy. The real Cathy. I'm betting you've been getting a bunch of text messages from my phone, which you were too stupid to figure out weren't actually from me. You've been had by my evil twin, moron."

Infuriatingly, I was crying. *Goddamn it.*

"Anyway, your dad just tried to throw me off a third-story balcony for refusing to marry him. Maybe you don't really give a damn, but you could at least stop emailing me hate-o-grams, okay?" I took a deep breath. *Hang up,* I told myself. *Stop now, before it gets messier.* "And Victor, if you're going to marry Jun, you could have just told me and let me beat the crap out of you, you . . . oh, hell," I said, sobbing. Then I hung up.

Still Life

It was almost three o'clock by the time I got home. Mom
was still sleeping. The house was quiet in the drowsy summer
afternoon. I was fairly sure the key to the post office box my
father had given Dr. Parkinson as his contact address would
be up in his studio. Back in the good times, after the post
office decided to turn one of his paintings into a stamp, he'd
converted part of our attic into a studio. He put in skylights
and big windows to let in lots of light and laid down a pretty
hardwood floor. We didn't have a lot of money, so he did all
the carpentry and wiring himself. We were amazed, but he said
he'd worked construction for a while when he was a young
man. My mom commented that apparently he had never spent
time as a dishwasher.

I hadn't been up to the studio since the day I found his body.

I sat at the bottom of the narrow stairs for what seemed like a
long time. Then I went up. Late afternoon light flooded through
the big studio windows and gleamed on the hardwood floors.
Scores of paintings finished and unfinished were stacked against
the walls. The room smelled faintly of oil paint and turpentine.
My dad kept his brushes in recycled jam and pickle jars; they still
stood in a line along the windowsill. The studio was bright and
full of silence, a still life by Vermeer or Claesz. My father's empty
easel stood beside the window. He'd pushed a thumbtack into the
easel's wooden top as a place to hang his key ring. The keys were
still there, brass and bronze and silver, their bright metallic colors a
glinting highlight in the composition of the room.

"Still life." What a lie. Life isn't still. Death is.

I grabbed the keys and wiped the tears off my face and went
downstairs.

The Key (Hour of Gathering Evidence)

By four o'clock I was at the post office with my dad's ring of keys. My hand was shaking again, so the keys clinked together, whispering secrets with their little metal tongues. I got out the smallest one and slid it into the lock on the PO box. It fit.

Inside I found a jumble of odd papers, including an ancient parchment scroll written in Spanish and a transcript of some poor SOB getting interrogated by the Inquisition. On top of everything else, as if it had been left there most recently, was a note.

> Thanks for the loan. I'll pay you back soon, I promise. And, of course, you have my promise that your family never has to hear about any of this.
> —David

I stared at this, completely confounded. The note sounded friendly and intimate. If there had been any doubt remaining that my father really did know Parkinson, this seemed to kill it. They were friends, or at least acquaintances. That would seem to swing things around to Jewel's theory that my father had enlisted the crooked doctor in a plan to fake his own death. But if that was true, what about the detailed scientific notes on the file in Parkinson's computer? Those really had seemed like the thoughts of a would-be poisoner.

And what about "thanks for the loan"? My mom would have gone ballistic if she had known dad was loaning money. But what if "loan" was a polite euphemism for blackmail? We knew Parkinson had tried his hand at extortion before. The more I thought about it, the more that seemed to explain. The doctor knew something—something *your family never has to hear a word about*." He tried to blackmail my dad, asking for a "loan" in exchange for his silence. He got the money, but then maybe he had second thoughts. Maybe he started to think about turning that loan into a permanent gift by murdering my father.

Of course, blackmailers who kill their victims tend to run out of money.

I stood in the post office feeling my brain begin to twist and sputter like an egg dropped into a hot skillet. Well, when faced with a challenging analytical situation, I always had one foolproof response.

Ask Emma to figure it out.

The Cathy Show (Hour of Broken Dreams)

The moment the elevator doors opened on the fourth floor of Emma's apartment building I could hear her and her dad arguing in Chinese. I almost turned around and left, but that would have meant I had wasted bus fare. I didn't have that kind of money to throw around.

I put my ear up against the door and listened. Mr. Cheung was doing most of the shouting. I had never heard him yell at Emma before. It was scary. It also made me mad. As far as I was concerned, he had abandoned his right to give Emma any

116.

crap the moment he put a thirteen-year-old girl on a plane by herself and sent her to the far side of the world.

At least having a stranger in the room ought to turn down the volume on Papa Cheung. "Hey, it's me," I called out, knocking on the door. There was a sudden silence, after which Mr. Cheung bit off a few choice words in Chinese. "Emma? Have you got a couple of minutes?"

Emma opened the door a crack. She looked shockingly pale and her face was tight and tired. "You look like crap," I said. "Are you okay?"

In the background Mr. Cheung added another salvo of bitter Chinese. "I don't think this is the best time for us to talk," Emma said, choosing her words carefully. "I have to sort some things out."

Guilt stabbed me in the chest. "It's Tsao," I guessed. "He told you he was pulling out of DoubleTalk?"

"Because of you!" Mr. Cheung said, appearing behind Emma and stabbing at me with a finger.

"Papa, investors have their reasons," Emma said. "It's just business."

"Business my ass," Mr. Cheung's face was ugly with rage. "He say very clear. 'Cathy can't come this, Cathy can't come that.' Very important man, but Emma's *friend* treat him like dirt. Important man has face."

My pulse sped up. *Crap, crap, crap.* Tsao was going through with his threat, and though Emma's dad was wrong about the reasons, he was right about the essential fact: Tsao was wiping out DoubleTalk because of me. "Emma, I am so sorry," I said. "I don't know what to say."

"You pick up the damn phone and call him and say you

117.

sorry," Mr. Cheung suggested. "You say it not Emma's fault, you spoiled little bitch."

"Papa!" Emma snapped.

I couldn't give Tsao what he wanted, but at least I could do something to pacify Mr. Cheung. I kept my voice humble and contrite. "If you think that would help, I'll make that call right now."

"Honestly, you've done *quite* enough already," Emma said. "We're fine. We'll get by."

"Emma, if there's anything I can do—"

"Now? No, there's nothing you can do now," Emma said sharply. "I kept begging you and begging you to come with us, Cathy. A free trip to the opera—you couldn't do that once in a while? You couldn't find time to come out for a free meal? That surprised me," Emma said. "That was a first."

A quick sting of shame there; me wondering if I had really mooched off Emma way more than I had invited her over to our house. I had the sick feeling I probably had. "God, Emma, I'm sorry," I said.

"Yeah, you say that a lot," Emma said wearily. "Honestly, right now I just don't want to hear it."

"All the time you use Emma," Mr. Cheung said bitterly. "Math? Emma does homework for you. School project? Emma does school project."

Keep your mouth shut, Cathy. Don't lose your temper, I told myself. But underneath the spike of outrage was another slap of humiliation. Mr. Cheung hadn't been around for all those math assignments and school projects. There was only one way he could have gotten the idea that Emma had carried me at school, and that was if Emma had said so. "Is that what you told him?" I asked her. "Is that what you really think?"

Emma didn't answer.

"You get in trouble, police come here," Mr. Chueng said. "What you give her? Nothing! Tsao make company, maybe make her husband. You don't care. What is Emma husband to you? What is Mr. Cheung sleep in street to you? Nothing."

"Yeah, that's what you're really pissed about, isn't it?" I said hotly. "*One* of us was sponging off Emma, that's for sure. You're just sorry to see your meal ticket go."

Emma took off her glasses and polished them on the bottom of her shirt. "Leave my father alone," she said.

I bit my lip hard. *Shut up, Cathy. Shut. Up.*

I had that sick feeling you get when a friend is about to ditch you. This wasn't a shouting match between two teenage girls. In some ways, Emma hadn't been a kid in a long, long time. Now she looked grown-up and tired, as if I was part of a past she had outgrown. "You aren't the only person who cares about me, Cathy. Sometimes I'm not sure how much you do."

"Is that what you really think?"

"You don't mean to wreck things for me," Emma said wearily. "You're just so busy being the star of *The Cathy Show,* you know?"

"That's not how I—"

"Can you just shut up for one minute?" I bit my lip and nodded. "You know what was nice about Tsao?" she said. "At least he listened to me, Cathy. When we were talking, he never made me feel like I was just some extra in the movie of your life."

That was too much. I had a vivid flashback to being in the mall, tipping slowly over the atrium rail, trying not to scream as I stared down at the marble floor three stories down. "Tsao never gave a damn about DoubleTalk!" I yelled. "He was stalking *me,* right from the beginning, okay? That's why he invested in DoubleTalk in the first place."

Emma went very still.

"Ok, here we go," Mr. Cheung said sarcastically. "Cathy Show again."

I rounded fiercely on him. "This afternoon, Tsao said I had to sleep with him or he would destroy DoubleTalk. And, oh yeah, he tried to murder me, too."

"Sure, sure," Mr. Cheung said, clapping his hands lazily together.

I was shaking with fury. "Fine. Maybe I should call Tsao back and hop in the sack with him. God forbid I let a little squeamishness get between you and Emma's first million."

Stiffly Emma said, "I never planned to marry Tsao."

"Maybe you didn't. *He* sure as hell did," I said, gesturing angrily at Mr. Cheung. "Come on, Emma—not even you can be stupid enough to miss that. 'Please, Emma, Mr. Tsao is here for dinner, so please put on your pretty dress! And for God's sake, let's get that Pete out of the room.' So what if *he* actually *likes* you—he's not an Individual of High Net Worth, so to hell with him."

"Is that what you think of me?" Emma said wonderingly. Her eyes searched my face. "I never knew."

"Oh, God. Emma, no, of course I don't!" Every angry feeling in me went out like a smashed light. "I didn't mean that the way it sounded. I am so…" *sorry*, of course. But there was no point in saying it, because Emma was right. Sometimes sorry wasn't enough.

120.

"You liar!" Mr. Cheung said. "Mr. Tsao see my daughter. Emma have something you never have, is brains!"

"Papa, shut up!" Emma closed her eyes. "Of course Cathy isn't lying. Of course it's about her," she said, voice flat. "It always is."

"Emma, I didn't mean it like that!"

"It's not like I'm stupid," Emma said, as if I hadn't spoken. "I guess I knew, really. He was always asking about you. Always wanting you to come along. Maybe I knew, but I told myself…" She shrugged. "I guess I just wanted something to be about me. For once."

Her eyes were dry and her face was expressionless, of course. Emma was a survivor. She had survived her mother's death and she had survived being left on her own at the age of thirteen. She would survive having her dreams betrayed by her best friend, too, although surely I couldn't have said anything more devastating. Not with a week to rehearse could I have driven the knife home any more cruelly. "Emma, I'm going to make this up to you. Whatever it takes, I'm going to make DoubleTalk happen. I'll buy stocks. Something."

Emma looked up at me with a ghost of a smile. "Cathy, you can't keep a job flipping hamburgers. As your financial advisor, I can't let you waste money on a start-up."

"What are you going to do?" I said humbly.

She shrugged. "I dunno. Go to school, I guess. I have a partial scholarship. Tsao isn't the only investor in the world."

"Damn straight," I said.

"Like hell," Mr. Cheung said. "You think it so easy? You think you get lots chances?" Where Emma was pale, his face was darkly flushed with rage. "Chances like bus, miss one, get

121.

next one? Not so easy. You just a girl," he told Emma. "You got idea, nothing else. Money don't give a shit about idea. Money give a shit about money. We out of chances, Emma. Time grow up. Real life is you go school maybe six months, then money gone," he said. "You get job at bank, maybe teller at bank, and that all. That what you do. I stay with you, I can't get no job because I don't speak English."

"Papa!" Emma started to say something in angry Cantonese but he cut her off. Whatever he said went into her like bullets and finally the wet shine of humiliation crept into her eyes.

"Emma, don't listen to him," I said urgently. "You are special, more special than I will ever be. Things are going to work out for you, I promise you. I swear it."

"I've had enough of your promises," Emma said. Then she shut the door in my face. I stood in the corridor outside my best friend's apartment. When I heard her turn the lock, I left.

Pepper Spray (Hour of Desolation)

After having almost fallen from a third-story balcony, and then breaking up with my best friend, I figured the day couldn't possibly get worse. I was wrong.

At first I was too devastated to feel anything but grief and shame. But by the time I got off the bus near my house my brain was working again and I was starting to get scared. Tsao had moved with savage speed to destroy DoubleTalk. I was pretty sure that was only the beginning. If the story on Auntie Joe's website was true, he was perfectly capable of stalking me, kidnapping me. Murdering me. I remembered tipping inexorably over the atrium rail at the mall, Tsao's hand on my back and the sick swimming terror in my chest.

Given how fast he had moved to crush Emma, there was a chance that Tsao or a henchman would be waiting for me when I got back to the house. What if a couple of his thugs were already going through my underwear drawer or tying my mom to a chair? What if someone was waiting for me behind the front door with a pair of handcuffs and a roll of duct tape?

I turned onto my street and walked slowly toward home, staying on the sidewalk opposite our house. There was no sign of the Mercury in the driveway. Mom must have already taken it to work. Good. I slowed down some more and scanned the street for any sign of Tsao or his minions.

Bad news. There was a Camaro parked across the street from my house. A guy in a dirty wifebeater shirt was sitting inside it staring at my front door. My heart rate sped up and my mouth went dry. I kept walking.

Get a grip, Cathy. He's probably just some local dude waiting to pick up a girlfriend or a buddy. Just walk around 123. *the block for a couple of minutes,* I told myself. *When you get back to the house, he'll be gone.*

Great theory, but five minutes later the Camaro was still there, and the thug inside it was still watching my house. He had a buzz cut and a two-day growth of stubble. His face was nicked up with a selection of scrapes and scars, some old and some still raw, the kind of marks you get from broken bottles and chair legs and being thrown into chain link fence. His upper arm was as thick as my thigh and ropy with muscle. It sported a screaming hawk tattoo above the words **Die Trying**.

In the movies, assassins are always smooth and wear expensive suits. Quiet as ghosts, they screw silencers onto

Die Trying

their guns before shooting their victims with minimal fuss. This guy looked like he'd charge you a hundred bucks and a case of beer to beat someone's head in with a brick.

Oh, boy.

I ran through my options.

Option #1. Call the cops. Problem was, what would I say? There was no law against parking a dirty Camaro on the street.

Option #2. Call in other protection. Normally, this is what boyfriends are for, especially immortal ones with superpowers and stuff. Unfortunately, mine wasn't even returning my email, let alone risking life and limb for me.

Option #3. Wait for Emma to figure out a Cunning Plan. Not happening today, and maybe not ever again. Which left the one option I really really hated:

Option #4. Deal with it yourself.

I kept walking to the end of my street, turned right, and made for the gas station a couple of blocks away. While I walked I waited for my courage to come back, but that didn't happen so I went into the gas station and bought a package of powdered sugar donuts instead. Licking the powder off my fingertips I decided that bravery was overrated. Sometimes sugar is just as good. I threw away my wrapper and coughed meaningfully to catch the attention of the pimply-faced clerk who was surreptitiously reading a copy of *Penthouse Letters* under the counter. "Hey," I said, smiling brightly. "Can I pick up a can of pepper spray?"

"We're out."

"Out?"

He tore his eyes away from his magazine and lifted them to somewhere below the neckline of my t-shirt. Not finding much there to hold his attention, he glanced all the way up to my face. "Yeah, all gone." His eyes went back to the magazine in his lap. "Sorry."

I had a brief but intense fantasy about pepper spraying him in a memorable part of his anatomy. Sadly, no amount of daydreaming was going to get Camaro Guy off my curb. I scanned the counter, on the off chance that they might be selling disposable flamethrowers or land mines or something. No such luck. Instead they had the usual crap: nicotine gum, diet pills, breath freshener (the spray kind), beef jerky (original recipe, teriyaki, and new Spicy Habañero flavor), *TV Guide,* Chapstick, candy bars, nail clippers, miniature flashlights, playing cards, and lottery tickets. "Fine," I said, grabbing a can of Cool Peppermint Mouth Mist. "I'll take one of these."

"Good choice."

"What the hell is that supposed to mean?" I said, but the clerk's attention had drifted back to his magazine. I added a tube of Krazy Glue to my purchases. There's always a use for Krazy Glue.

I sat on the sidewalk outside the gas station and studied my options. In the absence of pepper spray, I figured the next best thing would be the *appearance* of pepper spray. I considered my little aerosol can of Cool Peppermint Mouth Mist. The can was basic black aluminum, about the size of my thumb. Taking the sticker off was easy. Making it look like it was stuffed full of pepper spray was going to be more difficult. I had my usual random assortment of art supplies in my bag, but painting on the can with watercolors was obviously impractical, and a few quick trials made it clear that pastels and lipstick both smeared too much. I had some drawing inks, but they wouldn't fix on

125.

CONVENIENCE
CHIC

· Don't use when vice-
principal is also downwind
of air vent.

· Don't use in crowd.
(e.g. Junior Prom)

TIPS:

the metal. Nail polish gripped better, but it was hard to do crisp, threatening graphics in either Seashell Pink or Premium Plum, which is what I had in my purse. So I used a pair of nail scissors to cut a blank white page out of my sketch pad and Krazy Glued it to the can. Once I had a surface to work on, I started to draw.

At this point, it would be reasonable to ask why I didn't just keep walking around to different gas stations until I found one that stocked pepper spray. Three answers:

1. The next gas station was half a mile away, which is short in a car but long on foot,
2. Arts and crafts projects always calm me down, and
3. The only other time I had tried to use real pepper spray, it hadn't gone well.

I went for a wasp motif, painting black and acid yellow stripes on the can and etching **PERVBLASTER PEPPER SPRAY** in angry red lettering. It might not stand up to scrutiny on a store shelf, but clenched in the fist of an angry woman, I figured it would look convincing enough. While waiting for the ink to dry I put on some blue eye shadow and a little too much mascara, doing my best Jewel imitation and feeling tougher every time I examined myself in my compact mirror. Then I headed back for my house, feeling absurdly better. I had my tough-chick eyeliner and my gun-fighter's fitted vest. Sometimes all it takes is the right costume and props to make you feel brave. After all, why do you think superheroes fight crime in facemasks and pantyhose?

I approached the Camaro from behind and stomped up to the driver's side. The window was rolled down. "Looking for me?" I snarled.

The goon did a double take. "What the hell are you—"

"Shut up," I said, reaching through the window to shove my can of PervBlaster up his nose. "If you so much as look at me funny I'm going to turn your face into bubbling Cajun gumbo."

"Whoa, there." Up close, the thug looked even bigger and stronger. Blocks of muscle shifted as he lifted his palms in surrender. "You got the drop on me, cowboy." He squinted at me over the top of my can of pepper spray. To my disappointment he didn't look even a little bit terrified. "Now what?"

Good question. "Shut up," I said, just on general principle. "Who sent you? Were you supposed to kidnap me?"

"Goddamn," he sighed. The eyes looking at me over my can of PervBlaster were brown and bloodshot with fatigue, and he smelled like it had been a few days since his last shower. The Camaro wasn't a bouquet of roses either. It was littered with fast food wrappers and empty convenience store coffee cups. *This dude has been living in his car,* I realized. No wonder he was willing to do a little dirty work for cash and no questions asked.

"Honey, you are having a bad trip," he said in a Soothing Voice™. "The stuff in your head, it's not really happening, okay?"

"Nice try. I am not stoned," I said. "You were trying to kidnap me." Keeping my can of PervBlaster pressed close to his face with one hand, I dug around in my purse with the other and dragged out the Blackberry. "But if you aren't up to anything, you won't mind me calling the police then, will you?"

"No cops," he said sharply.

"*Aha!*" I cried. I groped around for the Call button on the Blackberry, couldn't find it, and risked a quick peek down at the screen. The instant I dropped my eyes his hand came

128.

GUNSLINGER GIRL!

up and slammed mine into the top of his car. I squealed and dropped my can of Not Actually Pepper Spray. The rent-a-thug jerked my arm half out of its socket, so my head and shoulders shot through the Camaro's window and I got a mouthful of steering wheel. His blocky fingers tightened around my wrist like a pair of pliers. I had the nasty feeling that he could crush my wrist like a peanut in a vise if he wanted to, and he was pretty close to wanting to.

"No cops," he said.

"I'm going to start screaming," I said. I tried to remember if it was Rape or Fire you were supposed to yell. In California, probably fire. You want the neighbors to think their landscaping might be at risk.

"*I don't want to hurt you,*" he snapped. "I'm just allergic to cops. I have parole issues. Let me guess—you live there, right?" he said, nodding at my house.

"No!" I said. I heard a car come squealing around the corner and brake to a stop across the street. "Listen to that," I gurgled into the steering wheel. "There's witnesses all around us! Help!" I burbled into the steering wheel. "Fire!" The car door across the street slammed shut. "*Help! Fire!*"

"Jesus." Camaro Guy shook his head in disgust. "Jewel sure can pick 'em," he said, letting go of my wrist.

My head turned inside out.

"Wait."

If this was Jewel's brother, technically that would be good news. It would mean I wasn't about to be kidnapped and killed, for instance. On the other hand, it would mean I had not only lured the guy halfway across the country by pretending to be his sister, but then tried to mace him and call the cops.

129.

Talk about no good deed going unpunished. "Aha," I began, with what I hoped was a charming girlish laugh. I turned my head in an attempt to make eye contact, but mostly just found myself staring into his heavily muscled armpit. "This is embarrassing. You're Denny, aren't you? And you weren't trying to kidnap me."

His armpit hairs fluttered in the breeze as he threw his exasperated hands into the air. "No kidding, Sherlock," he said. "Uh … you can get your head out of my car now."

Smackdown (Hour of Boys Being Boys)

Just as I started to apologize to Jewel's brother, a hand touched me from behind and time froze. "Cathy," the owner of the hand said, "step away from the car." It was Victor.

Without waiting for an answer he pulled me gently upright and set me to one side, graceful as a dancer swinging his partner on a ballroom floor, only much, *much* faster. Then the car door was open and Victor was hauling Jewel's brother out of the Camaro. "I don't like hearing this lady calling for help," he said softly.

"I don't know what the hell it is about California," Denny

said hotly, "but I've about had it with psychos coming into my goddamn car and—"

Denny swung in the middle of his sentence, a fast street-fighter's punch with a fist that would have splattered my face like it was made of wet concrete. He had lived on the streets and he was wicked quick, but Victor could have read a book waiting for the punch to land. He was in that special place where time slowed like syrup around him. The killing place. I couldn't even follow how he caught Denny's hand, stepped into him with a hip, and spun: but suddenly Denny was face down on the concrete, roaring with pain and anger. He scrambled upright, bleeding from his mouth. He was tough and he was mad, but he didn't have a hope in hell against Victor. Victor wasn't human and it wouldn't even be close. "Denny," I said. "Don't."

"You stay the hell out of this, skank."

Victor's eyes narrowed. "You'll need better manners after I break your arms," he said. "If you want people to bring you stuff, you have to ask them nice."

"Victor, stop! Don't kill him!"

Victor shrugged. "If you say so. If he dies in the ambulance, though, that's not my problem."

"Bring it on," Denny snarled.

Two tenths of a second later Denny's upper body crunched through the Camaro's window and his face hit the steering wheel hard enough to make the horn blare. "Victor!" I screamed. "Look at me!" Victor glanced around. "Good dog," I snapped. "Now play nice."

"Cathy, the guy was pulling you into his car! What the hell are you yelling at *me* for?"

"Hey, Kung Fu," Denny said thickly from behind us. "Try

this, you son of a bitch."

Victor turned around and Denny let him have it square in the face with Cool Peppermint Mouth Mist. The two men froze. They sniffed.

Time, which had slowed, began to smell minty fresh.

Both guys turned to look at me. "What the hell?" Denny said.

Victor sighed and rubbed his face. "Cathy, this whole scene is beginning to have your trademark … scent to it," he said. "Care to explain?"

Iodine

"You. Sit," I told Denny, pointing at the edge of the bathtub. "First, we have to get you cleaned up."

"You mean none of those text messages were from you?" Victor said, pacing around our downstairs bathroom like a leopard in a very tiny cage.

"Goddamn it, you broke one of my teeth," Denny said gloomily, wiggling it. He had muscular hands with engine oil stains around his fingernails. His palms were badly scraped from trying to break his fall when Victor slammed him to the street. He ran his hand through his military buzz cut and his fingers came up sticky with blood. "Got a cut up here, too. Wonder when that happened?"

"Scraped the frame when I threw you through the window of your car," Victor said absently.

Denny grunted. "Thanks for that, uh…"

"His name's Victor." As I dug through the medicine cabinet, getting out Tylenol and gauze and iodine, I kept glancing back at the guys. Something about them made a profound contrast, something my artist's eye was picking up but my brain couldn't put into words. Victor was well toned, quick and lean; Denny was stocky and more heavily muscled. But there was another difference between them, something more profound.

Ah. *Time.*

Nobody knows better than a portrait artist that time marks us—it nicks us up and leaves us looking used, like a well-traveled suitcase or a favorite book. Denny was only a year or two older than me, but life had left a lot of fingerprints on him. The broken tooth and split lip Victor had given him would be new additions to the chronicle of little scars on his face. There was a strange dent in the ball of his right thumb, a memento from some knife fight or car crash or workplace accident. One of his ears had been hit hard enough and often enough to be deformed, like the beginnings of a boxer's cauliflower ear. And of course there was the **Die Trying** tattoo. For the first time I thought about what an intensely human act it was to get a tattoo—taking an image or a slogan, some stray momentary emotion, and cutting it into your body so that it could never heal and never be erased.

Unless you were Victor. If you were Victor, time never left a mark, and the tattoo artist's needles would pass over you in vain, the words disappearing as if written in water.

"Cathy?" Victor said. "Are you all right?"

"What? Oh, sure. Just spaced out there for a second."

"Mm," Victor said. His expression of frustration deepened. "I already sent you a thousand dollars, you realize."

"You didn't send it to *me*. Jewel just ripped you off, sucker. A-ha! Iodine," I said, pulling my mother's trusty brown bottle from the medicine cupboard underneath the bathroom sink.

"Anyway, you can always put a stop payment on the check, can't you?"

"You said—I mean, Jewel said she needed cash." He paused and gave Denny an unfavorable look. Denny shrugged. I guessed this wasn't the first time he'd taken crap on his sister's behalf.

I grabbed a clean white washcloth and soaked it in iodine. As a kid I skinned pretty much every inch of my body falling out of trees and off bicycles and into rose bushes. I ought to have had the whole first aid thing down, but in fact I was a bit hazy on the details. The main thing I remembered from my mom was to be firm, crisp, and fast.

"Caller ID said it was you," Victor said morosely. "How was I supposed to know it was some lying little bimbo?"

"Hey," Denny said sharply. "That's my sister you're talking about, jackass."

"You mean she isn't a lying little bimbo?" Victor said unpleasantly. "The facts seem pretty clear."

"*I* can call her whatever I want. You keep your mouth shut."

Victor resumed pacing. "A brother's love. How touching."

"Hey, he drove thirty straight hours to come bail her out of trouble," I said. "You couldn't write me one crummy email when I needed help."

"I told you, she said I shouldn't trust the email account!"

"If you want to make back boyfriend points, you don't want to be dwelling on the fact that you couldn't tell the difference between a text message from her and a real email from me." A trickle of blood from the cut on Denny's head ran down the side of his face. I wiped it away.

"Do you have a plastic bag or something I could borrow?"

Denny said, holding up his bloody tooth. "I don't have a pocket in this shirt. Anyway, when do you think Jewel is going to show up? I just want to pick her up and get the hell out of this state before another random stranger attacks me."

"Jewel is coming here?" Victor said, perking right up.

"Um," I said, rinsing blood out of the washcloth. It would be convenient if the whole business of me pretending to be Jewel never came up, convenient here being a word which means "not exposing me to justifiable ridicule and scorn."

"This is where she said she was crashing," Denny said. "Usually she's staying with a guy when I pick her up. This isn't really her style. I mean, you're kinda skanky, but the house is…"

"Clean?" I said, slapping the iodine-soaked rag on the cut in his scalp.

"Holy cats!" Denny yelped "What is that stuff? Lighter fluid?"

"It's good for you," I snapped.

"Cathy, I still don't understand why you think Jewel would come here, after she stole your stuff," Victor said relentlessly.

I reached deep inside myself for hidden reserves of ArtGirl Mind Control Rays and beamed them directly at his head. *Drop the question, Victor. You live only to worship Cathy, -athy, -athy … !* "Yeah, well, let's not worry about all that," I said brightly, rinsing out the washcloth again. "Why don't we give her a call and you two can arrange a rendezvous and go back to Texas and everyone can live happily ever after."

Victor gave me a long, steady look. "I know that voice," he said. "That's your Distracting Victor voice. It makes me realize you never actually answered my question. Why is

135.

Jewel staying here? Or … she isn't, is she?" He stopped his pacing. "If she was, you wouldn't have told me to cancel my check—you would have said we could get the money from her when she showed up here."

"Jewel said she was staying at this address—" Denny stopped abruptly. "No, she didn't exactly say, either," Denny said slowly. "She sent me a text message. Just like she did to Kung Fu here."

"Or maybe it wasn't Jewel who sent those messages," Victor said. His mouth started to twitch into a smile.

Busted. "Um," I said again, dribbling another shot of iodine onto the washcloth.

"You mean … Jewel never did write me?" Denny said slowly. "That stuff about how I shouldn't join the army, how people would give a crap if I died … she never said any of it?"

"Uh, that would be me," I said. Gently I wiped the cut next to his mouth. "Denny, troops are dying every day to stay in a country where nobody wants us." Up close, in the bright light of the bathroom, I could see all the little nicks and scars in his face—the map of a hard life, maybe even a brutal one. I wondered how many of those battle scars had come defending Jewel, or his other half-sibs. I wondered how many had come at the hands of his mother's string of worthless boyfriends. "People need you," I said. "Just because it wasn't Jewel who wrote those things, that doesn't mean they're not true."

Denny looked up at me. His expression was hard to read. I tapped his hands and he turned them over. I looked at the poor flayed skin of his palms. "Some gravel in here," I muttered. "I'll have to take that out with tweezers. OK: this is going to sting." I spilled iodine over his bloody hands and dabbed at

136

them. He drew in a sharp breath but didn't complain.

A funny thought flashed through my head: if I stayed with Victor, I would never do this for him. I had seen a bullet go through his chest and watched the hole film over with new skin in the time it would take a normal person to put on a Band-Aid. If we stayed together, Victor would see me turn my ankle, or cut my hand in the kitchen—maybe someday even watch me go through labor. Years after that, there would be a clogged artery, or diabetes, or a tumor … sooner or later he would hold my hand while the doctors told me how long I had to live. When the time came and I took my last breath, I would not in all those years have done as much for him as I was doing for Denny right now with my washcloth and bottle of iodine.

I found a plastic bag for Denny's broken tooth and a wad of cotton to swaddle it in. He wrapped up the tooth and stuffed it in the pocket of his jeans. I found the tweezers. "Give me your hand." Obedient as a schoolboy, he stuck out his palm. I studied the bits of grit embedded in it. *Calm,* I told myself. *Brisk. Businesslike.* I took the tweezers and pushed them slowly into his hand. It took some fiddling to get the little steel arms around the first sharp pebble, and when I tugged it out, Denny winced. "Did I hurt you?" I said anxiously.

"Hell, yes." He smiled at me. "But thanks." I couldn't help smiling back.

When I turned to rinse out the rag, Victor was watching us.

You Have To Break A Few Eggs (Hour of Melting Butter)

Once Denny was patched up, I herded the guys out of the bathroom and into the kitchen. The kitchen is my favorite part of our house. Dad painted it bright lemon yellow, and Mom put cheerful curtains on the window over the sink. I think it was the room they were happiest in together, chatting over breakfast coffee or washing up after dinner, back before Mom worked the graveyard shift. The kitchen was also where food came from, which made it a big deal in my life all the years I was growing up. "Denny, when was the last time you ate?"

"Do Cheetos count?"

"When was the last time you ate *food?*"

Denny ran his hand over his buzz cut, feeling where the short bristles of hair were still tacky with blood. "I had a hot dog at a gas station just outside Phoenix, I think. Seems like I got something in Nevada, too. An order of hash browns or something."

"You can't keep all those muscles by eating a box of hash browns once a state." I opened the fridge door and pulled out a carton of eggs. "Omelettes OK?"

"You're very Suzie Homemaker today," Victor remarked.

Denny frowned. "I didn't come here to eat up your food."

I grabbed a mixing bowl. "Pride is one thing, stupid is something else."

Denny started to protest, but Victor cut him off. "You want to get a shot of breath freshener in the eye? Take my advice: if you want to cross Cathy, you gotta learn to pick your battles."

I grinned. "Damn straight."

I like making omelets. My dad taught me when I was

little, maybe eight or nine. His theory was that precise measurements weren't really my long suit, so I should learn to cook something that had a lot of artistic license in terms of ingredients, and also involved breaking stuff. He said that mixing an omelet was a lot like mixing paint: the eggs were my basic palette, and then I could build tastes out of whatever ingredients I had around. Rooting around the fridge I found some cold sausage patties left over from my mom's breakfast, a clove of garlic, a Tupperware container of cold canned corn, half a cup of congealed fondue, and three packets of salsa left over from take-out Mexican food.

Perfect.

Denny kept poking his tongue around the hole where his tooth used to be. "I've fought some guys who were fast before but, *damn,* Victor. Where'd you learn that kung fu?"

"I was in the military," Victor said. Strictly speaking this was true, although he left out the part about having joined up to fight World War I.

"Really? I was thinking of enlisting," Denny said.

"Which is idiotic." I peeled the clove of garlic and chopped it up. "You spend all day riding around in a jeep waiting to hit a land mine, and at the end of it maybe you machine gun some fifteen-year-old girl you hope was a terrorist. And that's a *good* day." I looked at Victor. "Right?"

"Well," he said slowly. "I suppose that's true … but it's not the only thing that's true. People die in war, yes. But everyone else dies, too. It just takes some of them a little longer."

"How very Ancestor Lu of you," I said, slapping a little skillet on the stove. I put the cup of fondue in the microwave to make it liquid again and then I took out six eggs and broke

Mom had made it from a mix to celebrate my new job the night before I got fired.

139.

them into the bowl. The eggshells crunched and buckled like little skulls. I wondered how many people Victor had killed. Not just with machine guns, but up close.

I beat the eggs and then chopped up the breakfast sausage and added that. "Most people die years before their heart stops beating," Victor said. "They get trapped like crabs inside the shell of their own habits."

The microwave pinged. I took out the fondue mix and poured it in with the eggs. It smelled of sharp cheese and some kind of booze. I put the salsa in, too.

"As far as being a soldier, I guess some people find themselves, and others get lost. You won't be the same afterward, that's for sure. Sometimes you get to a place in your life where you're so desperate to change, that's enough." Although he had never talked about it directly, I had pieced together enough of Victor's past to know he had enlisted after his first marriage went disastrously wrong.

I put a pat of butter into the hot skillet and watched it come apart.

"My probation officer says I don't tend to make real good decisions," Denny said. "I figured maybe I'd let somebody else take a turn."

I brushed the garlic into the skillet off the cutting board and the smell crept through the room. I remembered pictures from Iraq, angry mobs and the crackle of guns and buildings burning. Giant columns of flame heaving and roaring. Tiny people running through the streets. I poured Denny's omelet into the smoking skillet. The edges writhed and hissed, bubbling. "So you're going to need a place to crash," I said, flipping Denny's omelet, then sliding it onto a plate and passing it to him.

Victor raised an eyebrow at me. "You have a suggestion?"

"As a matter of fact, we do have a couch," I said icily.

Denny looked up from his omelet and grinned at Victor. "Worried?"

"How's your head feeling?" Victor asked silkily.

Denny laughed and forked up another mouthful of eggs. "No worries, man. I'll find a place."

I poured the next omelet into the skillet. "What do you want him to do, Victor? Sleep in the Camaro?"

Denny paused for just a second. "Yeah, well, I've done that once or twice," he said.

Death of an Immortal

"Cathy!" The front door banged open and Emma came running in. My first reaction was, *Thank God, she forgives me!* but her face was shocked and serious.

"Emma! I'm so glad you—"

"No time for that," she said. "I'm still not interested in being part of The Cathy Show, but the fortune-teller is dead and I thought you should know."

Victor's shot up, sending his chair clattering backward. "What do you mean, dead? That's impossible."

"Hi, Victor. Aren't you supposed to be on a table somewhere getting your kidneys removed?"

141.

"I've missed you, too," Victor said.

"I had a Google alert set for LuckyFortuneForYou. It went off about fifteen minutes ago. 'Eccentric Psychic Found Dead.' A maintenance worker found her body in a Dumpster, but not in St. Louis. Here, in the Bay Area." Emma watched me. "But maybe that part isn't such a surprise to you?"

"I saw her earlier today. Listen, are you sure she's dead? Not just … pretending?"

"She'd have to be a really good pretender," Emma said. "Someone with a camera phone shot a few seconds of video as the rescue workers got her body out of the Dumpster. He posted the footage online. You can hear the cops saying she had been strangled."

"That's impossible," Victor said again. And it should have been. Auntie Joe was an immortal, like him and Tsao. She should have recovered from choking effortlessly. I had a sudden flashback to the odd thing Auntie Joe had said when she'd saved me from Tsao at the mall. *Just cuz Auntie Joe can see the future, that don't mean she can change it.*

"She knew," I breathed. Auntie Joe had known she was going to die. Of course she had. She had come to California to save me, knowing that she would be murdered.

I felt sick.

How long had she known? Did she know she would die for me when Columbus sailed for America? When Charlemagne was crowned? My head was spinning.

"There's more," Emma said. "The person who uploaded the video caught the cops talking. Apparently they found a few strands of—"

"White silk," I said.

142.

Emma stared at me. "How did you know?"

"Lucky guess." I looked at Victor. "Jewel stole the scarf you gave me."

Denny dropped his fork with a clatter. "Jewel wouldn't kill nobody. Well, maybe one of Momma's boyfriends," he said. "Not some old lady."

"Well, someone did, and they used the scarf she took from my room."

"If the murderer was smart enough to wear gloves," Victor said slowly, "he can leave a 'tip' for the cops any time he wants, telling them where to find the scarf … and telling them to test it for your fingerprints and DNA."

"Bloody hell," Emma said. "It's a frame-up. It's Tsao. He's got the scarf, and he's going to use it to blackmail you. You can't stay here," she added. "He'll find you here, or the cops will. Come crash with me."

"Emma, your dad would smother me with a pillow if I tried to crash at your place." *And I wouldn't blame him,* I added to myself. "Plus, it isn't the most subtle hiding place in the world, is it?"

Emma looked at me over the tops of her little round glasses. "First place the police would look, I should hope," Emma said. Which I took to mean, "I forgive you."

"First thing anyone would tell them about me—Emma's best friend," I said. My eyes were misting up. "Emma Cheung's number one fan."

"I should hope so," Emma said crisply. "But that still leaves us with the problem of where to stash you."

Denny winked at me. "There's room in my Camaro," he said.

Good-bye (Hour of Forever)

"This is all extremely … interesting," Victor said. His eyes were distant. Part of him was already far away, locked into tactical mode. "Cathy, I think I have to go now. There are things I need to discuss with Ancestor Lu." His voice was clipped and brisk, a soldier's voice. "I need a pen." I got him one from the drawer under the microwave and he wrote something quickly on the back of a card. "I need to talk to you alone."

"We can go out on the porch," I said.

It was well past eight o'clock, and outside the long summer twilight was deepening. Kids had all gone in for dinner. The blue glow of TVs flickered in the picture windows of our little suburban street. Someone at the end of the block was having a barbecue; you could hear snatches of laughter and smell the smoke, charcoal tinged with lighter fluid.

Victor handed me the card. It had an email address on it. "If you don't hear from me in three days, write this address. I'll try to leave word for you there," he said. "But promise me you won't write before that."

I put the card in my back pocket. "If it takes you three days to get back to me, you're in big trouble, mister," I said, trying to make a joke.

"Yeah," he said. Not joking at all. "Listen, Cathy. There is nothing between me and Jun. I would never betray you that way."

I meant to say thank you, but it came out, "Why not?" A crow beat heavily overhead, going about his secret business. "I mean … it just makes sense. You said it yourself—sooner or later I'm going to abandon you, Victor, just like Bianca did. I'm going to grow old and ugly and finally I'm going to die."

More crows passed by, three, five, many of them, stroking

A single crow swims
through lonely dusk. Who can tell
His destination?

over the rooftops, veering around the live oaks and the Chinese
pistache and the sycamore trees.

Victor cupped my head in his hands and kissed me, a long
kiss. "God, I've been wanting to do that," he said, while I
scrambled to get my breath back. "Cathy, do you think an
immortal can really be in love?"

My lips were still tingling with the touch of his mouth. "I
hope so," I said.

"I try to remember what it was like, before I knew I couldn't
die. It was such a long time ago." He took my hand, running
his thumb lightly over the back of it, skin whispering over skin,
as if it was the only warm thing in a cold world. "What I felt
for Giselle, for my sister Franny … I think that was love. It
hurt like love." He shook his head, frowning. "I was watching
you with Denny just now," he said abruptly. "And I found myself
wondering if it was selfish of me to keep you. A mortal life…"
He trailed into silence. Cicadas started to buzz in the dim
evening air around us, the sound gathering and fading away,
fading and gathering.

Victor looked at me with troubled eyes. "Your life is a
journey to a destination I can't even imagine. I can give you
a lot of things, I can give you money and safety and all my
heart … but maybe that isn't what you really need." He stirred,
looking out into the dusk. "Maybe company on the journey is
the only thing that matters."

The last thin edge of the sun slipped into the sea and darkness
seeped into the valley. "I do know I will love you forever,"
Victor said. "And forever, for me, is a very long time."

I kissed him again before he left.

145

Cathy's Key (Hour of Emma's Forgiveness)

Fifteen minutes later I was riding in the passenger seat of Emma's BMW, the one that she was going to have to take back to the dealership for the second time this summer.

"Are you still mad at me?" I asked.

"Yes."

"I don't mean it to be The Cathy Show," I said.

Emma grunted. She was driving very fast, as if the car had to match the speed of her thoughts. "Did you leave a note for your mother?"

"Yeah." I looked nervously at the speedometer.

"Good."

"I told her I was spending the night at your place so we could talk about designing my website." As soon as the words were out of my mouth I winced: Emma working on my website: somehow I had made it all about me again.

"Yesterday I had a plan," Emma said morosely. She swung out into the fast lane, doing well over eighty. The BMW's halogen headlamps pushed sleek ribbons of asphalt under us. "Now I don't. School, I suppose, but then what? I only have a partial scholarship—I'm going to have to get a job. How can I keep up my GPA if I'm working on the Geek Squad at the local Best Buy?" Emma waved her hands around in a way that you'd really rather someone driving at that speed wouldn't. "And afterward, what about investment capital? Let's face it, the Chinese cell phone market might be all parceled out by the time I graduate, even if I get through my coursework in three years. So what do I do then? Without access to capital, will I become just another leveraged buyout analyst for some investment banker? A brand manager for a yard goods

146.

company?" She turned to fix me with a Look of Woe ™.
"Even business school majors have dreams, Cathy!"

"Lane!" I squeaked, as the Beemer chattered rhythmically
over the lane dividers. "Left lane or right, Emma. Pick
one, please."

Emma drifted into the fast lane. "Entrepreneurs, Cathy!
That's where the adventure is. Start your own company, turn an
idea into a product the world wants—that's spinning straw into
gold, you see. That's the dream," Emma sighed. "Plus obviously
there's more economic upside." We seemed to be cruising on the
highway shoulder now. "Hey, was that a raccoon?"

"Emma! Focus, please!"

"You don't have to get all hysterical," she said huffily.

I held my breath and counted to eleven. "So, where are we
going?" I grated.

"Oh. Pete's place."

"Your programmer?"

"Yeah, he lives down at the marina—oh, bloody *hell!*"
Emma grimaced. "I have to tell him his stock options are
worth less than a roll of toilet paper."

"Well, less than two-ply maybe," I said. "They've got to
be at least as valuable as that single layer stuff they put in the
Greyhound station."

"Gee, thanks," she said.

"Emma, I'm really sorry about what happened with Tsao,"
I said. "Your dad is right about one thing: I do take you for
granted sometimes, and I really don't deserve you."

"That's two things."

"Also, I'm not good at math."

"Apparently not." Emma swerved around a pickup truck

147.

and blew past the startled driver. "Do you remember the first time you came over to my place?"

"Eighth grade science project. The egg drop. You made us Mac & Cheez for dinner."

Emma laughed. "Right! We were supposed to drop the egg off the gym roof without it breaking, and I wanted to make all these elaborate protective cages to put the egg in … and then you said, 'let's put it in a chicken.'"

I grinned, remembering the long, expressionless stare she had fixed on me. "Hey—Mother Nature's original egg-protection packaging."

Emma glanced over at me and smiled and I smiled, too, but then I looked away. I was desperately grateful to be friends again, but the speedometer needle was drifting north of 85 and I really needed her to watch the road.

"My point is that you were there that night," Emma said. "My dad wasn't." Black asphalt unwound underneath us and the BMW flew down it toward the sea. "The thing is, Cathy, he needed me to learn to live without him. So I did." She swung out of her lane again and passed another car, leaving its lights to dwindle behind us, shrinking, shrinking, and then gone, cut off by the crest of a hill. "If he doesn't like it now, well … he got exactly what he paid for, didn't he?"

I didn't know what to say.

Emma drove in silence. The lights of San Francisco gleamed and sparkled below us. "I got the stuff from my dad's post office box," I said at last. "I remembered seeing the little key on my dad's key ring."

"You do notice things," Emma said. "That's the key, I think—*hey!*" Emma jiggled her foot enthusiastically on the

148.

gas pedal. "CathysKey.com. That's a *great* URL for your website! It's perfect! Like Victoria's Secret, but in an A-cup." I punched her in the shoulder. "For a very modest management fee, I will run this online gallery gold mine," Emma cackled. "Plus web hosting fees and site maintenance, obviously."

"Emma, could you *please* slow down?"

Emma whooshed around a Porsche dawdling along at 80 miles an hour. "Slow down? Kid, I'm going to make you a star!"

www. cathys key . com

The Moonshine (Hour of the Peppermint Schnapps)

"Pete lives on a boat?" I said, staring at a twenty-foot craft with *Moonshine* written on the hull.

"I told you he lived at the marina." Emma leaned over from the edge of the dock and banged on the side of the boat. "*Moonshine*, ahoy!"

"Yeah, but … this isn't even a houseboat, it's just a *boat* boat. Not even a big one."

"Yeah. Pete's dad is a bit … odd," Emma said cryptically. "Pete says staying here is less weird than being at home."

A tangled clump of hair rose through the forward hatch. "Emma? And Cathy! Did you steal something?" he asked, interested.

"No!"

"On the run from the law?"

"Sort of," I admitted. "Look, I'm awfully sorry and I know this is short notice, but—"

Pete cut me off with a wave. "Hey, you already made me break into some confidential files, and swipe a biometric keypad with a stoned doctor's hand," he pointed out.

149.

"Basically, you're just living up to the hype."

"Can I pick 'em?" Emma said proudly, stepping off the dock and onto the rocking deck of the *Moonshine*. "An eye for personnel is an executive's most important asset."

"Plus he works for free."

"That, too."

Pete clambered onto the *Moonshine*'s deck and held out a hand to guide me into the boat. "And I'm not working for free, I'm working for stock options."

Emma and I exchanged a look. "About those stock options..." Emma said.

Pete's smile turned wry. "Ah." He helped us onboard and then led the way down to the tiny cabin below decks. Emma filled him in on DoubleTalk's disastrous day while Pete filled a small kettle from a jug of drinking water in the tiny kitchenette. "We have tea, coffee, or hot chocolate, ladies."

Emma and I both agreed that this was a hot chocolate situation.

The main cabin was no more that six feet high and eight feet long. A long cushioned bench curved to follow the line of the hull; it obviously doubled as Pete's bed. The other "wall" was lined with an impressive and unexpected array of scavenged electronica. As Emma explained about Tsao, DoubleTalk, and the fortune-teller's death, Pete flipped open his laptop and scanned the web for details of the crime. "You think Tsao *killed* this woman?"

"Killed her, or had her killed." I shrugged. "He's very used to getting what he wants."

Pete scratched his head, worried. "Yeah, but … what he wants is *you,* right?"

150.

The little kettle whistled. Emma poured hot water into a pair of mugs and then stirred in packets of instant hot chocolate. "I've been thinking about DoubleTalk, and really, I was going about it all wrong," she said, handing me my cup of cocoa. "What could I bring to the Chinese cell phone market that was really unique?"

Pete, sitting on the other side of Emma, gave me a quick wink and went back to scanning his computer. "So, what's next? You just wait to see if the cops come after you?"

"I guess." I probably should have mentioned the police in the note I had left for my mom.

"You're going to have to do clothing on Cathy's Key," Emma said thoughtfully. "Art by itself doesn't really sell, at least not at first. In the early years we'll need to find a way to monetize your talent. T-shirts, obviously. Sweatshirts. Ball caps. You can come up with designs that look good on a ball cap, can't you?"

"Emma, I haven't really given it any thought—"

"This is why you need a manager," she said tartly.

Pete's fingers danced over his keyboard. "Do you know where Tsao lives?"

I blew on my hot chocolate, shaking my head. "He gave me a business card once, but it just had a phone number for an office in New York. Where he stays when he's in San Francisco I just don't—*ack*!" I spluttered. "Emma! What did you put in this hot chocolate?"

"Peppermint flavoring!"

"Uh … peppermint schnapps," Pete said, looking a little alarmed. "My dad likes that stuff. I use it to take the rust off stuck bolts."

Dear Mom
Sleepover at
Emma's Place
xxx ooo
P.S. If the cops
show up with
a list of charges
Don't worry—I'm
not guilty of the
bad ones...

151.

"You put booze in our hot chocolate?"

Emma rolled her eyes. "The bottle just said peppermint. Think of it as peppermint mocha and don't be such a baby," she said impatiently. "Let's talk about thongs."

"Thongs?"

"Thongs?" Pete said, momentarily distracted.

"Look, it's not as if I would ever wear one, but I think they are trend-right with your target demographic," Emma said seriously. "You can do a design that looks good on a thong, can't you?"

"Emma!"

She frowned. "Something *narrow*, obviously…"

1086 is a Great Day in the History of Banking, as it marks the compilation of the Domesday Book, the first comprehensive Excel spreadsheet. <smile> Other dates obviously acceptable.

Identity Theft

Within a few minutes Emma had downed her hot chocolate and polished off the last half of mine. The three of us were sitting on the bench with Pete in the middle trying to figure out where Tsao was staying. "Do you have his social security number?" Pete murmured.

"Are you kidding? He was my primary investor. Last four digits were 1086. Now, wait, that's my new—never mind. Anyway, I have the DoubleTalk investment documents by heart," Emma said. "Heck, you want a credit card number? I kept a running total of his business development expenses so I could pay him back when we were solvent," she added bitterly.

A little swell moved under the *Moonshine,* wake from some supertanker passing through the harbor. Emma swayed with it, closing her eyes.

"You wouldn't happen to know the password for his credit card accounts, too, would you?" Pete said jokingly.

"Thirty million dollars," Emma murmured sadly, bumping into Pete's shoulder and then rocking away in the other direction. "Was that so much to ask?"

I blinked. "I know the password for his voicemail account. Would that help?"

"Really?" Pete said sharply. "Now we're in business. Most people reuse passwords."

Another wave brought Emma back to sag against Pete's shoulder. "I just don't understand why it's always about Cathy," she mumbled. "What's so great about her?"

"Emma, I'm right here," I said.

Emma opened her eyes and stared up in the general direction of Pete's ear, blinking owlishly. "Jus' because she can break and enter? Is that it? I can do that," she said with a sad hiccup. "I'm an *outlaw.* Bandito Cheung. Can do things with an Excel spreadsheet, make gangbangers cry like little girls. Bang, bang!"

"Emma—"

"Shh." Pete grinned at me and held a finger up to his lips. "So how did you figure out his voicemail code?" he said quietly.

"Tsao has a thing for diamonds. He puts that shape on all his stuff—business cards, what have you. The voicemail asked for a four-digit code, and Emma had the idea that maybe you could try the numbers that made the shape of a diamond on a telephone touchpad—2-4-8-6."

154.

"Whoa." Pete looked down at Emma, still lolling against his shoulder. "She's pretty smart when you keep her away from the schnapps."

"Cigarette lighter and a tube of Krazy Glue, I could be Cathy," Emma mumbled. "But nope. Nobody ever pays attention to Emma." She began to slide slowly down Pete's shoulder. "Nothing exciting ever happens to mmmmm…"

Pete was on the credit card site. "Identity theft," he murmured. "Not just a hobby, but a way of life."

"What are you hoping to find, exactly?"

"This!" A credit card statement flashed onto the monitor and Pete quickly highlighted a (staggeringly large) hotel bill. "Tsao is staying at the Montgomery Arms." He pulled up the hotel's website in another browser window and scanned for their room rates. "Judging by these prices, he's in the penthouse suite."

"Nice! For once I have the drop on him."

As my dad used to say, an army marches on its stomach. No, wait—wrong motto. I can't remember the way he used to put it, exactly, but the sentiment was that it was better to start kicking someone else's ass than waiting around for them to kick yours.

Emma was now completely slumped over and snoozing on Pete's lap. "I don't think she should drive home," I said. Emma's head lolled over to one side, and she made a teeny tiny snore, just once.

Gently Pete shut down his laptop and set it aside, careful not to disturb the girl asleep in his lap. "There's a hammock I can rig down here to make a second bed. I'll take my sleeping bag up on deck."

"Outside?"

66 — The best defense "" is a good offense.

God is on the side of the big battalions?

"Sure. I've done it before." He looked down at Emma, reluctant to disturb her. It was warm in the little cabin and her face was flushed.

"She's usually not like this," I said. "I'm the flaky one."

"You like her a lot, don't you?" Pete said.

"Yeah."

Emma grumbled, shifting into a more comfortable position.

"Me too," Pete said.

Clip-Clop, Clip-Clop (Hour of the Mysterious Messenger)

Clip-

Clop.

Clip-

Clop.

Clip-Clop. Clip-Clop.

Clip-Clop.

Clip-Clop.

Pete frowned. "Who would ride a horse onto a dock?"

"Not a horse, the hoofbeats aren't heavy enough." A tingle of anticipation spidered down my back. "It's something lighter."

"Like a cow?" he said. "Okay, that makes sense. People ride *cows* onto the dock all the time."

Clip-Clop, Clip-Clop, Clippity-Clop. The hoofbeats stopped next to the boat. "If I were guessing," I said, "I'd guess that was a donkey."

A moment later there was a rustling, flapping, rattling sound. The boat lurched to one side as someone stepped onto the deck above us. I reached across Pete's lap to shake Emma by the shoulder. "Come on, Emma. Wake up. You said nothing exciting ever happens to you? Here's your chance. It's Paper Folding Man!"

"Glb, glb, mmph," Emma said. Her eyebrows squinched into a frown and she curled into a tighter ball.

The topside hatch creaked open. A moment later, a paper bird came winging down the narrow stairs. It fluttered impossibly around the cabin, flapping its origami wings, and then bumped gently against me, hovering in the air. I caught the paper bird in my hands. It struggled and fluttered against my fingers as I opened it up and read the words painted on it. "Memorial for the Fortune-Teller. Hitchcock Mausoleum, Cypress Lawn Cemetery, Colma. Tomorrow at 11 AM There will be someone there you should see—but don't be seen!"

As soon as I read the last word, the bird sighed, and rustled, and lay still between my palms, ordinary paper once more.

156.

Unexpected Business (Hour Too Damn Early to Have a Name)

In my dream I was a seasick dolphin caught in a tuna net. I woke to find real life pretty much the same. I was tangled in the mesh netting of Pete's hammock, swinging a couple of inches from Emma's nose in the dim cabin of the *Moonshine*. The boat was rocking at anchor; presumably another big tanker had passed by, and the swell had woken me up. The brass-bound ship's clock read 5:17, but the pale blue digital readout on the microwave read 4:58. Averaging those figures, I came up with Too Damn Early.

My teeth were furry, my hair needed washing, and I had that seedy feeling you get when you sleep in your clothes instead of changing into PJs like a good girl. I wanted a shower like a drunk wants a forty-ounce can of malt liquor. I struggled to something like an upright position in the hammock and smacked my head against the ceiling in the process. My face felt funny, and when I ran my fingers over it, I could feel little grooves from the hammock lines imprinted on my cheeks.

Just another day in The Cathy Show.

Getting up proved to be another episode of slapstick comedy, rated PG-13 for graphic clumsiness and coarse language; it ended with me clinging to the hammock's underside like a spastic opossum. From there, it was but the work of a moment to drop heavily to the floor, where my landing was cushioned by Emma's hot chocolate mug. There was a small splintering noise which might have come from my spine.

For a moment I lay very quietly in the darkness. Partly I was silent because I didn't want to wake Emma up. I was going to a memorial service for a murdered immortal, and I

157.

didn't want her coming with me. I had dragged her into more than enough trouble already, and there was no way I wanted her anywhere near Tsao. To her, he was a traitorous business partner who had tried to put some moves on her best friend. She had never seen an immortal kill, never truly experienced how little they cared about human life. She would want to confront Tsao, because she just couldn't comprehend that he would snap her neck with no more compunction than he would swat a mosquito.

The second reason I lay mute in the bottom of Pete's boat was that I'd had the wind knocked out of me. That didn't seem especially noble, however, so I decided to concentrate on what a good friend I was while waiting for my spasming diaphragm to come back online. I've had a lot of experience in getting the wind knocked out of me after jumping off things, falling into things, or occasionally being run over by things. I know the drill. When I finally managed to drag air back into my lungs with a suppressed whoop, I spent a few seconds enjoying oxygen again and then crept on my hands and knees to the short, steep ladder leading up to the *Moonshine*'s deck.

When I poked my head up through the hatch it was cold outside, and foggy. Over the sea it was still dark, but the gray morning light was beginning to work its way down the streets of San Francisco. The first cars were beginning to crawl through the streets; the first gulls were beginning to wing lazily around the harbor, looking for bits of last night's garbage that might have gone undetected in the dark. The dark blob of Pete's sleeping bag lay stretched like a six-foot slug across the *Moonshine*'s forward deck. Presumably Pete was cocooned inside it, waiting to emerge in another hour like a tousled, hyperactive butterfly.

158.

I tiptoed carefully over the sleeping bag, clambered over the ship's rail, and stepped onto the dock. No sign of anything stirring in Pete's sleeping bag; no muffled questions from Emma below decks. Mission accomplished. Now I had to hike back into the city, find a BART station and either see if the trains would take me out to Colma, where the memorial was supposed to be, or get me home where I could borrow the car, since Mom would be at home sleeping during the day.

I walked quickly up the dock toward land, wishing I was wearing more than a plain cotton shirt. Mark Twain wasn't kidding when he said, "The coldest winter I ever spent was the summer I spent in San Francisco." Halfway up the dock I was already starting to shiver. I picked up the pace until I was almost jogging as I ran off the dock and into the parking lot at the marina.

The door of a parked car swung open. "Man," Denny said, "you're in some kind of hurry."

Like many strong and powerful women suddenly confronted by the unexpected, I jumped backward and made a little squeaking noise. Jewel's brother grinned at me from the front seat of his Camaro.

"Are you stalking me?" I spluttered.

"What are you going to do about it? Throw mouthwash on me?" He turned the key in the ignition. "I didn't have any particular place to be, so I followed you and your friend. Somebody ought to suspend her license, by the way."

"She was upset." I meant to sound haughty and aloof, but I was suffering from second degree fogburn and my compulsive shivering sort of ruined the effect.

"Looks like you're running out on her."

"I was just stretching my legs—"

"My whole family is pretty good at sneaking off," Denny said. "I figure I recognize the signs." He squinted, peering more closely at me. "Did someone hit you in the face with a tennis racket?"

"Shut up," I said, trying to scrub the hammock lines out of my face.

"Look, I need to find Jewel," Denny said. "You're my best chance of tracking her down. For your part, you look like you could use a ride. Why don't you get in and we'll grab some pancakes and see if we can make a deal?"

"Does your p-probation officer know you've left T-texas? Seems like a quick call to the cops would get rid of you p-pretty fast."

"Have you filed a stolen property report on that scarf of yours?" he shot back. I glared at him and my teeth chattered in what I hoped was a scornful manner. "There's a heater in the car," Denny said.

Some arguments are too powerful to resist.

Denny pushed an assortment of drink cups and fast food wrappers off the passenger seat and onto the floor. I got in. "Okay, Cathy, how much money do you have for breakfast?"

"Uh… eight bucks?" I said. "Better call it two—I'm going to need money for the train."

"OK, well, I'm going to be following you all day," Denny said, adjusting his rear view mirror. "So if you ride around on the subway, we both have to buy tickets. That will leave you with enough money for drive-thru Tater Tots for breakfast. Or, you could let me drive you wherever you're going today, in which case if we pool our money we have enough to eat diner

160.

waffles." *Mmm. Waffles!* said my treasonous stomach. "I like the ones with the strawberries and whipped cream on top," Denny said.

"I could always go back and get a ride from Emma."

"You have a death wish?"

The Camaro's heater was finally beginning to work. I huddled up as close to the vent as the seat belt would let me. "Okay, you win," I growled.

"I haven't been on a date in a while," Denny said as he put the car in gear and pulled out of the parking lot. "At first that tennis-racket face of yours was disturbing, but now it's kind of turning me on."

"Whoever told you 'smug' was attractive was lying."

Denny grinned. "All I know is that your boyfriend skipped town and you're sitting in my car."

"Shut up and find me breakfast."

Colma (Hour of the Wrong Place to Be When the Zombie Armies Attack)

After a breakfast of waffles and diner coffee, Denny and I cruised over to Colma, where the memorial service for Auntie Joe was to be held. In 1900, San Francisco passed a law banning cemeteries within city limits. This in turn created Colma, an incorporated city less than two square miles in size, 73 percent of which is made up of graveyards. Not only was anyone who subsequently died in the Bay Area likely to be planted in Colma, but they dug up the nice folks already buried around town and shipped their remains to Colma, too. As a result, the population of Colma is roughly 1,500 above ground,

161.

and 1.5 million more below. That's a thousand to one, if you're keeping track. Emperor Norton is buried at Colma, along with Joe DiMaggio and William Randolph Hearst.

They don't import a lot of fertilizer.

A pretty ironic location for a gathering of immortals, I was thinking as Denny drove us there. On the other hand, to an immortal, I guess, the whole world is Colma, isn't it? If you live a thousand years, I suppose every city feels like a cemetery first and a community second. Time is long, death is patient, and the ghosts will always outnumber the grieving.

The immortals were due to arrive at the Cypress Lawn Memorial Park at the grave of Lillie Hitchcock Coit. Lillie spent her life obsessed with fire, was an honorary member of the fire brigade, and after she died left vast sums of money to build Coit tower—shaped like a fire nozzle. I'm not sure exactly why the family felt she needed a big mausoleum; Lillie, unsurprisingly, was cremated.

Denny and I found a nice spot to spy from behind a smaller mausoleum. We were out of the fog belt, and the day was turning warm. There was a copse of cedar trees behind our hiding place. The bright sunshine dipped their edges in light, and filled the air with a faint odor of dust and heat and pencil shavings that reminded me of my father's studio.

A solitary figure walked up from the road toward the Hitchcock Mausoleum, followed a minute later by another. Slowly the immortals arrived. Pretty soon it was clear that Emma was right about the genetics of immortality; only half the people coming seemed to be Chinese.

As the immortals gathered, birds were arriving, too, singly or in pairs, flitting and darting among the cedar branches.

162.

Crows, at first, but then as time went by other birds as well.

My father had painted birds. We had a facsimile edition of Audubon's *Birds of America* downstairs, and a coffee-table book of the brilliant J. Fenwick Lansdowne's paintings. Looking up into the branches I was surprised at how many birds I could still name: common ones like the crows and mockingbirds and scrub jays, but I saw a solitary vireo and a Say's phoebe, an American goldfinch and a hooded oriole and a Lazuli bunting, too, which was the last bird my dad ever painted.

It's the day before my father's death and he is showing me his new painting. "I finished your portrait," he says, teasing.

I look at the chubby blue bird with the cinnamon chest and white bars on its wing. "This is supposed to be me?"

Picking up a reference book he clears his throat and reads, "An energetic, beautifully colored bird, the lazuli bunting's call is a high, rapid, strident warble."

I punch him in the arm. Not hard, just enough to let him know I'm practically a grown-up now, not just the little kid who used to worship him. He laughs and I go downstairs. In a few minutes Emma will call me up and invite me over for the night. I will never see my father alive again.

"What's the matter?" Denny whispered.

I scrubbed a couple of tears off my cheek. "Nothing," I said. "I just like birds."

Slightly Displaced in Time (Hour of Revelation)

Fifteen minutes later, Victor arrived with Ancestor Lu. He was wearing a nice suit and walking a respectful pace behind his employer, but he also seemed to be looking around a lot. Very possibly looking for me, come to think of it; Victor had experienced enough of both my mad stalker skilz and my getting-into-trouble superpowers to be nervous.

Of the other Chinese immortals, I recognized Paper Folding Man, who arrived leading a white donkey. There was also a beggar, terribly disfigured and missing one leg. I had never seen him before, but recognized him from research Emma and I had done as Iron Crutch Li. No sign of Jun, Ancestor Lu's estranged daughter. I wondered if Victor knew where she was.

There were also immortals I didn't recognize in the gathering. One was a wizened old man, very spry, with a long curly beard, a walking staff, and a small round hat. There was an enormously tall black woman with an ivory necklace, and also a short, cheerful-looking fellow who might have come from the Yucatan or Guatemala, brown-skinned with a wide-boned face and quick eyes. Each newcomer greeted the others carefully, sometimes with a few quiet words, more often with just a look and a nod.

Ancestor Lu walked forward to stand framed by the door of the Hitchcock Mausoleum. He turned to face the gathering. As another pair of crows flew squabbling into the cedar behind me, Tsao appeared from the direction of the parking lot, striding briskly with Jewel on his arm. She was wearing shoes with too much heel and the walk was problematic for her. She was wrapped in a black designer dress—Versace, by the cut—that was probably the most expensive piece of clothing she had ever

164.

worn, but it only made her look like a rich man's mistress.

The hawk tattooed on Denny's shoulder bunched as his hand balled into a fist. I grabbed him and mouthed the word "wait."

Ancestor Lu acknowledged Tsao with a short nod. "Thank you all for coming," he began. "Normally we do not need to meet. Normally, there is nothing left to say. Today is not a normal day. One of us has died." The air seemed supernaturally quiet; even the birds had gone still. "As most of you know, I have dedicated myself to ending unnecessary death. Some of you disagree with this aim," he said, with another polite bow to Tsao. "I wonder how many of you feel the same way today?"

A breath of wind muttered through the branches of the cedar as a straggler came hurrying up to the gathering. He was a middle-aged man with a bald spot, a bit on the thin side, not too coordinated; every part of him slightly awkward except his hands. The hands were beautiful, deft and wise: hands for steadying a bicycle, for pouring milk into a cereal bowl, hands for putting on Band-Aids and ruffling your hair. "I'm not late," he said, panting a bit. "Just slightly displaced in time."

I scrambled to my feet. "Daddy?"

Betrayed

Heads turned as I stumbled out into the open. Everyone was staring at me and I didn't care. All I cared about was my father looking back at me. He didn't seem happy to see me, or guilty, or ashamed. Just weary. "Cathy," he sighed. Infinitely tired.

His dead body, the smashed glass on the studio floor—it had all been a trick. The dim numb days. My mother turning old and bitter and drinking gin. All a trick. Just a fancy way to get rid of us. He was one of Them and we were just a situation he'd gotten tangled in and lied his way out of. Parkinson, the crooked doctor, obviously worked for several of the immortals. He had arranged a way for my father to "die," then showed up to wave off the EMTs when the ambulance came. Maybe they went out for drinks that night to laugh about it, my father and his accomplice. *"Did you see the look on that kid's face? Priceless!"*

I walked toward him, passing Paper Folding Man and the tall black woman and Tsao. "My daddy left me, too," Jewel murmured as I went by, "but at least he didn't pay for the privilege."

And there was nothing I could say because she was right. Exactly, precisely right.

"You're crying," my father said. I was so angry I hadn't noticed. I still knew every line in his face, the freckles on his forehead, the way his dark brown eyes tilted down just a little, making him look pensive even when he said he was just thinking. Spanish eyes, my mother had called them. Dark and sad. "I understand. I know you're angry, too, because that's what you do." He was talking, but it was hard for me to understand the words. The first shock was melting away. Deep down, some part of me wanted to collapse, wanted to die, but I did what I always do: I found the bright fury and rode it up. He hadn't shaved in a couple of days and a fine stubble was showing on his chin and upper lip, framing his mouth as he spoke. "All I can tell you is that I've tried staying before," he said. Anger was pounding in me. Roaring through me. "I had a daughter once who died because I didn't leave soon enough."

I hit him. The first time he let me and then I tried to hit him again and he caught my hand because he was one of Them and you can't ever hurt them. Not really. Not like they can hurt you.

"You *lied* to me!" I meant to say the words but screamed them instead. "You *lied*."

"Yes," my father said simply. "It's what people do. You know that, kiddo. You're a fairly good liar yourself."

I was furious, breathing hard. Rage crackled in my body like ugly lightning. "Do you know what happened to Mom? Do you know what it's like to sneak into the liquor cabinet every night and pour out a little bit of gin, just enough so she won't notice it's missing but the bottle runs out a few nights faster?" I looked at the sad-eyed man I had known all my life and it was like looking at a stranger. Everything I knew was wrong. There was still a wedding ring on his finger but it was costume jewelry now, just another part of his disguise.

Mom used to talk about how he was already going bald when she met him, but then he never got any balder and of course I should have noticed, but I hadn't. He'd even bought the occasional bottle of Rogaine and left it in the bathroom. All part of the charade. It was like finding out he'd been having an affair for twenty years, spending his weekends with a mistress and sending money to buy presents for her children. It didn't just hurt now. It made everything fake. It made my whole family a lie.

My father's voice was quiet. "Cathy, if it matters, out of all my children, you were one of the ones who meant the most to me."

I blinked. *Of all my children?* How many others had he had? One? Two? Dozens? Were any of them still alive? Did I have a half-brother or half-sister walking the earth somewhere? I wasn't immortal—at least, not yet, not

167.

according to the lab work Victor had done on me. I glanced at
Victor. He stepped toward me, and I could read in his face that
he would have done anything to spare me this moment. But
then, he had left families, too, hadn't he?

I turned back to my dad. "Wow, one of your favorite kids,"
I said savagely. "Great to know I made the top ten. You know
what? I'm going to tell the world about you—about all of you,"
I said, staring around at the immortals gathered on the cemetery
lawn. They looked back, curiously unmoved. I was crying so
hard it was difficult to see. "I'm going to tell Mom," I said.

"You sound like a nine-year-old," my father said. "I'm sorry,
Cathy, but you're going to have to be grown up about this."

"Don't you dare use that tone with me," I spat. "Only one
of us gets to be pissed off right now, and I'm thinking it's me.
Do you realize that at your funeral we—"

My father leaned forward and tapped me on the shoulder.
Time died at the touch of his finger and I was frozen in place
as if I had been nailed to the bright air. "Don't start on the sad
stories, Cathy. I've lived them all. OK?" His head was tilted to
one side and his lips were thin—the tight, angry look he used to
get when I interrupted him at work, or ruined one of his brushes.
"You think we haven't done this before?" he said, nodding at the
rest of the immortals. "You think you're special?"

My throat cramped and it was hard to talk. "I don't want to
hear this," I said. My anger turned small and hid. It was like
that kid feeling you get when you are sad or hurt or lonely and
you scream or cry to your parents and they _crush_ you with their
grown-up feelings. Rage as big as the sky. Loneliness like
an ocean you could drown in. Huge grown-up feelings that
annihilate you where you stand.

My father touched me under the chin and searched my face with those sad Spanish eyes. "I've played this scene a hundred times," he said. "I don't think you understand that yet. What it means. I've been a kind father and a deadbeat, a Good Samaritan and a monster. Some times I've gone a hundred years without a friend to keep from hurting people. Other times I've screwed my way through armies of whores and left bastards behind me like dandelion seeds." He glanced at Victor. "I've met my *one true love*, Cathy: not once but dozens of times. I've lied and I've told the truth, I've run away and I've stayed to watch the years burn her down like a match and blow her out. I've had kids, Cathy, dozens of them. Hundreds. Did you think you were the first girl I read a bedtime story to?"

"Please, stop," I whispered.

"But you want to tell me about your pain? Listen, Cathy, one day you are going to learn that time hurts, and that isn't something you can fix with the right eye shadow or a trip to the mall."

For the first time in what seemed like a century, another voice broke the stillness of the bright sad air. "That's a cheap shot," Victor said mildly. "That isn't the real Cathy, and you should know that."

"As for him," my father said, "how stupid do you have to be, knowing what you know, to let yourself fall in love with an immortal? I suppose you think you're so much smarter than your mother that you can find a way to make it work."

Victor took a step toward my father. He had his pocket watch tucked into the pocket of his vest, and the chain clipped to the opposite side swayed as he walked. I watched the light glint and flare on the steel links, because sometimes if you look

169.

at things very carefully you can hide your whole self in your eyes and keep from feeling.

"Leave her alone," Victor said.

"How many women have you had?" my father asked him. "A dozen? Couple of dozen? You're still very young. Have you spent a whole mortal lifetime with a woman yet? Maybe the two of you can try it. In a few decades you'll be fifty, Cathy, and putting on weight. Your hair will get thinner and start to lose its color. He'll still be beautiful, of course, and you will find yourself wondering what other pretty girls he's thinking about when he is kissing you. When he comes to your bed you'll wonder if it's out of pity … but maybe by that point, pity will be enough for you."

"Please stop," I said. Tears were running from my eyes like blood from a wound, leaving me weak and sick. As if I could die from crying.

Victor, still looking like a handsome, dangerous young man of twenty-three, faced my sad-eyed middle-aged father, who could have been forty-five years old, or four thousand. "I am not like you," Victor said quietly.

"You can't imagine what it's like to be me, Victor. But I have surely been you," my father said. "I have made every choice you ever made and all the ones you haven't yet. I know how the story turns out." He dismissed Victor from his attention and his dark eyes returned to me. "I hurt you, and I'm sorry, Cathy. But don't presume you've cornered the marketplace on grief. Because even this moment, this heartbreak? I've been through it a dozen times before, with children I loved every bit as much as I love you. I know how this story ends, too."

Silence. In the branches overhead, crows shifted, watching us.

I forced myself to speak. "What's going to happen?"

My father looked up into the cedars, as if studying the birds that had gathered there. "You aren't going to tell your mother, because all it would bring her is pain. You and I are going to go our separate ways, and you will always hate me a little, and you will always love me, and you will always need something from me that I can't ever give." One of the crows hopped from his branch and beat heavily into the sky, making for the bay. Another followed the first, and another, a line of black birds like mourners at a funeral, heading for the sea. "That's just the way it is," my father said.

My eyes hurt. My throat hurt. It was hard to talk. "You can't make me believe you don't love me," I said carefully. "I think you're trying to make me hate you. I think this is your way of trying to make it easier for me."

He looked at me, expressionless. "Even if I am, everything I said would still be true." The anger was fading from his eyes, leaving weariness and grief behind. "As for Victor . . . don't do it, honey. It just can't end well."

Tsao stirred, and a thin smile curved one corner of his mouth. "That is certainly true."

"And you," my father said, with a bright spike of real anger. "You stay away from my daughter."

Tsao shrugged. "It is a sad truth about this life: we don't always get what we want."

171.

Sister's Keeper (Hour of the Mortals)

"What a creep," Denny said. He came out from our hiding place and strolled up to join me. "Hey, Jules," he said. "Nice dress." He was talking to his sister but his eyes were locked on Tsao.

For once, Jewel was taken completely off guard. "Denny! What the hell are you doing here?"

"Looking for you. Like always."

"Get out of here!" Jewel bit off. "I can take care of myself."

Denny had come up to stand directly in front of Tsao. They were about the same height, but Denny outweighed Tsao by sixty pounds of muscle. He paused and spat deliberately to one side. "So, this the new date?"

Jewel's voice was uncharacteristically low. "Denny, I mean it. You're in over your head." She glanced at me. "Why did you let him come here?"

Denny grabbed Jewel by the wrist. It looked like an old familiar gesture, and I guessed he had dragged her home a hundred times before, at age seven and nine and seventeen, from playgrounds and swimming pools and bars.

Tsao placed his fingers ever so lightly on the hand grabbing Jewel. "Don't touch that," he said mildly. "It belongs to me."

Denny started to swing at him. Tsao broke his wrist first, then his elbow. The wrist happened so fast I couldn't see what happened, I just heard the sound, like a paintbrush snapping. Then Denny was on his knees with his arm stretched out, palm down, so his arm was straight out like a board. Tsao turned and dropped, smashing his right forearm straight through Denny's elbow. The arm snapped and tore. Then Tsao was standing calmly again. Denny writhed on the grass with his arm

172.

sickeningly bent the exact wrong way, as if his elbow had been put on backward. He screamed. Tsao kicked him in the face and the screaming stopped abruptly.

"Stop!" Jewel yelled. "He didn't mean it!"

Tsao looked down at Denny writhing in the grass. "I did."

He started to kick Denny again, but suddenly Victor had stepped between them. "Enough." A long look smoldered between them. Then Ancestor Lu barked out a sharp command in Chinese. Tsao stepped back and adjusted his shirt cuffs.

I dropped to the ground beside Denny. He was gritting his teeth to keep from screaming, but a clammy sweat had come out across his forehead. Victor knelt beside me. "We should get him to a hospital," he said.

I grabbed his hand. I wanted to tell him how grateful I was that he had spoken out for me. How much it meant to me that he could still care about us absurd, fragile, mortal people. I wanted to tell him that I was not my mother and we could be together without me being bitter and grim. Mostly I wanted just to close my eyes and be with him for a minute because he was the only person left I could trust with all the broken pieces of my heart. But I didn't have the words or the time to say any of those things, so instead I grabbed his hand and squeezed it.

And he pressed back, a light, certain pressure, and found my eyes, and time opened up like a cormorant's wings. Great spans of time uncurled between heartbeats for me, and sounds died. Overhead, birds hung motionless in a bright sky that smelled of light and dust and cedar trees. And Victor's skin against my skin was forever. *I see you,* he said, although he did not speak out loud.

My father's bleak, bitter words had made me feel fake,

plastic, empty. In that moment, if only for a moment, Victor made me real again.

Tsao's Bargain (Hour of the Truce Between Immortals)

Ancestor Lu said, "I would prefer to avoid further disturbance." His eyes met Tsao's. "Perhaps we can come to an understanding."

Tsao studied his shirt cuff where a spatter of Denny's blood had stained it. "Dry-cleaning," he said, annoyed. "An understanding. Very well." He glanced in my direction. "Lift your protection off her, and I will leave the other boy alone. In fact, I will go so far as to withdraw my objection to your ridiculous plan to bring immortality to the masses." All of the immortals looked up sharply at that. "I still don't believe this scheme is either practical or wise," he said, "but give me the girl, and I will withdraw."

"She's not property," my father said. "Nobody gives Cathy but Cathy."

"You shut up," I said furiously. "I don't want you talking about me."

"Fathers are always reluctant," Tsao said. "I've been that way myself. But consider this. The immortality gene isn't dominant in her, but she must be carrying it. Your daughter will grow old and die. But we might make grandchildren— ones you could know, and stay with, forever."

"Oh, yes," Victor remarked, glancing at Ancestor Lu, "immortal children. Look at how much comfort that has been to Lu Yan."

174.

"Victor, we've got to get Denny out of here," I said.

Victor stood up in front of Tsao. The family resemblance between them was unmistakable. "Michael Vickers is right. Nobody gives Cathy but Cathy herself."

"Victor does not speak for me," Ancestor Lu said. "His judgment is clouded by a personal interest. For myself, peace between immortals is precious. The girl is a small price to pay."

Victor sighed. "Then let me make her a little more expensive," he said, and he pulled something out of his back pocket and held it up for everyone to see.

It was a small can of Cool Peppermint Mouth Mist.

Mortality (Now in a Convenient Spray Can!)

"As everyone knows, it's easier to break something than to fix it," Victor said. "Several months ago, Ancestor Lu and I began an intensive biological research project. We wanted to find the key to immortality. A couple of weeks ago, we made a breakthrough." Right around the time he had snuck out to visit me at the Burger Barn, I thought. What had he said that day? *Ancestor Lu is very happy with me right now.*

"This discovery was not nearly enough to allow us to make regular people immortal," Victor continued. "But it was enough, as I mentioned to Ancestor Lu at the time, to make a serum that would disable the immortality gene in one of us."

The immortals glanced at one another, their faces marred by a tense expression that looked unfamiliar, as if they hadn't worn it in a long time. The expression was something like fear.

"When I heard that Auntie Joe had been killed, I

175.

immediately suspected that some of Lu Yan's other workers, unknown to me, must have been busily developing such a serum. I ran back to the lab at once—no doubt leaving Cathy feeling abandoned yet again," he said, looking at me, "for which I am genuinely sorry. To make a long story short, my guess was right, and the serum exists. How Auntie Joe came to ingest it, I don't know. Who killed her afterward I don't know either, though I have a guess," he said, turning back to Tsao. "What I do know is that I have an aerosol version of the serum with me at this moment, and I will have absolutely no compunction about using it on anybody who gets in my way."

Victor held up the "pepper spray" can I had tried to threaten Denny with yesterday. "Cathy is not going with the honorable Tsao Kuo Ch'iu. She is coming with me, right now, and we are taking this guy with us," Victor said, grabbing Denny's good arm and helping him to his feet. "The first person who tries to stop us gets to find out what it feels like to be mortal again."

"You okay?" I whispered to Denny.

His face was ashy with pain. "Nope. Not hardly."

"You came in a car," Victor muttered. "Where is it?" I nodded toward the lot. "Okay, let's go."

"You are making a choice you will live to regret," Ancestor Lu said.

"If the choice is you or Cathy," Victor said. "I choose Cathy." He looked at my father. "You should have done the same."

"Cathy," Tsao said softly. "Last chance. Victor is young. He cannot protect you. Your father; well, you know what you can expect from him," he said contemptuously. "I can protect you, and I will *never* leave you."

"Is that a promise, or a threat?"

Tsao spread his hands. "That is up to you."

"Okay, Cathy," Victor murmured, "time to go." He propped up Jewel's brother and guided him a couple more steps toward the parking lot. I tried to help support Denny without touching his mangled arm.

Jewel was still standing next to Tsao. Her face was a mask, expressionless. "You should come with us," I told her suddenly. "You aren't one of them." Jewel didn't move. "For Christ's sake, Denny came all the way from Texas to take care of you, and you're just going to stand there?"

Jewel looked at Denny's arm and then looked away. "I can take care of myself," she said.

The immortals watched us, uncertain as to what they should do. Tsao looked furious, Ancestor Lu thoughtful. Paper Folding Man watched the whole scene with lively interest.

My father said, "I didn't know you would be here today. I didn't want you to find out." Those sad Spanish eyes were weary, those fine hands helpless at his side. "I never wanted to hurt you, Cathy."

My daddy left me, too, but at least he didn't pay for the privilege. "What you did to Mom—that was unforgivable," I said. "You are going to live forever. For you, there's always another chance for happiness. Mom has only a little life. Thirty more years, maybe forty at the most."

Victor touched my arm. "We've got to go, Cathy."

My eyes were blind with tears. "A little human life is all she had, and you stole the hope out of it, you son of a bitch."

177.

"I think we've both hurt your mother," Dad said. "One of many things we share, Cathy."

"I hate you," I said.

LESLIE VICKERS

"She looked after everyone else but nobody looked after her."

Cool Peppermint (Hour of Getting the Hell Out of There)

We staggered down to the parking lot, me and Victor on either side of Denny. When we got to the car Victor reached into Denny's right pocket and fished out the keys to the Camaro. "Are you OK to drive?"

I took a deep breath. "I can do it."

He tossed me the keys. "Your problem is, you are way too brave for your own good."

I grabbed the keys and tried to wipe away the stupid tears so I could see. My nose was running, along with my remaining mascara and my tear ducts and my self-esteem; there was a lot of crap dribbling onto the Camaro's steering wheel, in short. I turned the keys in the ignition. "I don't feel very brave."

"Trust me on this one." Victor eased Denny into the back seat and then clambered in after him.

"Keep your hands to yourself," Denny panted. He was trying to make a joke, but his face was gray and lined with pain. He kept making little high-pitched grunting noises through his teeth, *unh-unh-unh*. Personally, if it was me with my arm snapped backward, I'd go ahead and scream. Jagged bits of bone had come out through Denny's skin when Tsao broke his arm and he was bleeding pretty heavily, a steady leaking drip that ran down his forearm and soaked into his white shirt and his jeans.

178.

"That's it," Victor murmured. "Way to hang in there, Denny. You are one tough hombre."

"Nah. Just had—*unh*—the crap kicked out of me—*unh*—a lot."

"I guess practice makes perfect." In the rearview mirror I saw Victor put his hands lightly on Denny's shattered arm. "Hang on, tough guy. I'm going to move your arm one time and use the seat belt to hold it in position so it's not quite so—"

"Ahh!"

"—likely to move around," Victor said. "I was an army medic once. I know this hurts like hell, but I've seen worse."

"Damn it—*mm!*—blood all on my upholstery."

"It's vinyl," I said. "It will wash off." The smell of Denny's blood was already filling the little car. I cracked my window to let in some fresh air and then backed out of the parking space.

"Cathy, have you got any painkillers?"

For *that?* I thought, but I tossed my purse into the back seat. "I think there's something in there. Root around."

"This all you got?" Victor said, holding up a bottle of regular strength Tylenol.

"I thought you were Mr. Medic. What did you bring?"

"Uh … one can of Cool Peppermint Mouth Mist," Victor said.

I stared at him in the rearview mirror. "You mean that whole speech about the Spray of Death was BS?"

He grinned. "Not quite. It was all true up to the part about me having the serum. They were making it all right, but I couldn't find where they were storing the stuff. I only found the lab where they were making it this morning. I could tell from the lab notes they had been working on an airborne delivery mechanism, so I figured that would be a credible threat."

179.

Three minutes ago I wouldn't have believed I would ever laugh again, but now a reluctant smile began to twitch my mouth at the idea that Victor had just stared down a group of the deadliest people on the planet with a can of Cool Peppermint Mouth Mist. "Denny, we're only about ten minutes from the hospital where my mom works. That's where I'm going to take you, okay? Can you hang in there?"

"Didn't have—*unh*—other plans."

"How's he doing?"

"Hmm," Victor said, in a tone that suggested Not Great. "Denny, you're starting to go into shock a bit, here. Try your best to stay awake."

"Bad news," Denny said. "Hurts like—*unh*—son of a bitch. Sleep—*mm*—sounds pretty good."

"Trust me, twenty minutes from now you will be loaded up on Vicodin or Percocet, or morphine if you're really lucky. That's the good stuff."

"Should have taken Jewel," Denny said raggedly.

"Jewel!" I said. "God, after that display, she deserves what she gets, as far as I'm concerned."

Denny grunted. "Not your—*unh*—sister. And he's not gonna treat her nice." *Duh*, I didn't say. "Momma had a boyfriend once," Denny rasped. "Was a son of a bitch. But he always used to—*mm!*—say: *nobody hits my little brother but me.*" The Camaro went over a bump in the road, and Denny closed his eyes against the pain. His breath was getting faster and more ragged. "If he touches her—*aah!*—I'm going back there with a gun." He stopped, gasping as another wave of pain rolled through the arm Tsao had destroyed so effortlessly. "Okay, maybe a rocket launcher," he added. "Or a flamethrower."

Emergency (Hour of Sneaking Off on My Own)

The nurses at the ER recognized me. I won't swear that made a difference, but I will say that a real doctor was looking at Denny within ten minutes of us walking in the door. Of course, he was pretty horribly mangled.

Victor took the nurse aside where Denny couldn't hear and offered to pay for a private room. Denny started to figure it out—he'd been in emergency rooms lots of times before, and was used to being stowed in a cot pushed against a corridor wall. But within minutes the nurses had an IV in his arm, liquid painkillers were dripping into his bloodstream, and he lost track of his pride.

I told Victor I needed to go to the bathroom and then walked quickly out of the hospital. I had been careful to keep the keys to the Camaro. Standing in the hospital I had found myself shaking pretty badly, looking at Denny's poor butchered arm. It felt much better to be out on the road. Something about gripping the steering wheel with a destination and a plan helped calm me down. Within two minutes I was on the 280 headed back to San Francisco and the Montgomery Arms hotel. I almost called Emma for the street address, but I figured that would just get me into the same long argument with her that I didn't want to have with Victor.

Right now, Tsao had my scarf—a piece of evidence he could use to turn the cops on me at any moment. Also right now, he was probably in the middle of a long and unpleasant conversation with Ancestor Lu and the other Immortals. I was never going to get a better chance to get into his room, steal my scarf back, and possibly find evidence that would clear me of Auntie Joe's murder. But experience had proven that selling

Emma on even the most justified and rational bit of break-and-enter tended to devolve into long, time-wasting arguments, and frankly, I didn't have the energy to spare. I called Information and got the address of the Montgomery Arms from them.

Just past San Bruno there was a dead dog on the side of the road. Hit by a car, no doubt. I watched the sad furry lump dwindle in the rearview mirror. We are all animals. We're born like them and we break like them and that's the truth at the bottom of things. We think we are special because we have produced Rembrandt and Pop-Tarts and infomercials, but death is our real common heritage. At the end of the day, I shared more with that dog than I did with Victor and Tsao.

OK. That's what I was thinking and it's true, but it wasn't the whole truth.

If I'm completely honest, the truth is that I was in a cold, sick sweat the whole time I was at the hospital, terrified my mother would show up. In my head I knew she was supposed to be at home asleep, but I couldn't stop thinking that she might have been called in for a special shift. Every second I was there I had the nightmare sense that she would come around the corner, she would look at me and she would know what Dad had done to us.

I had always loved him better. And the shame of that, knowing what I knew now, was more than I could stand.

The Montgomery Arms (Hour of the Secret Shopper)

The Montgomery Arms was a pricey boutique hotel a couple of blocks from Union Square. The lobby floor was black marble and the reception desk was ebony. On the desk were bunches of orchids with petals as black as Goth lipstick. The concierge had an air of effortless superiority, as if his night job was conducting the symphony or curing cancer. I half wondered if he would have me thrown out immediately, or perhaps instruct the beautifully uniformed footmen to shoot me on sight. I reminded myself that we were on the West Coast, after all, home of the dotcom zillionaire (official uniform: jean shorts, sandals, and t-shirt with pizza stains.) The main thing, I told myself, was to look like I belonged. Footmen can smell fear.

On the drive I had been turning over the question of how to get into Tsao's room. The maids presumably had "skeleton key" cards that would let them in. My thought was to make a scene outside the door, claim to have lost my key, and ask them to let me in. Against security procedures, no doubt, but I was hoping that I had one extra factor in my favor this time: they would have noticed a woman going in and out of Tsao's room, and that woman looked a lot like me.

The drawback with this plan was that the elevator wouldn't even go up to the penthouse floor. There was a button for it, but when I tried to push it, the elevator's LED display politely asked me to insert my room card in the reader for access.

Damn.

Well, if the elevator declined to take me where I needed to go, I could try the stairs. I took the elevator to the floor below the penthouse suite. Once there, I padded down the long,

expensively carpeted corridor to the emergency exit at the
end of the wing. I pushed the heavy metal fire door open and
found myself in the stairwell. It was the usual bare concrete
flight, but with tastefully recessed lighting and a painting on
the landing. Not an original painting—a print of a Turner
seascape—but still, you had to hand it to the Montgomery
Arms: class all the way.

The clock in my head was ticking urgently. Every passing
minute would be bringing Tsao closer to his suite, and I very
much did not want to meet him again today. Or ever. My
footsteps sounded unnaturally loud in the echoing stairwell
as I trotted up to the penthouse floor. The door was locked.
"Haven't you people ever heard of fire regulations?" I muttered.
No doubt the door had one of those one-way devices you could
push open from the other side.

I said a bad word but it didn't make me feel noticeably better.

I grabbed my purse and rooted through it, just in case I had
happened to stash some plastic explosive in with my makeup,
or perhaps packed a ladylike little arc welder in there, suitable
for cutting circles in steel doors. No such luck. All I had
was the usual collection of girl junk: a pair of sunglasses, two
ancient sticks of gum, my smallest sketchbook, and a selection
of drawing pencils. In other words, nothing.

Or … ?

Nobody was going to let Cathy Vickers up to the penthouse
suite … but they might let Jewel get there. Obviously, nobody
who knew Jewel well was going to think we were the same
woman. But I wasn't trying to fool Denny, here—I was
going to be dealing with the concierge, or possibly a clerk at
Reception who would only have glanced at her while dealing

with Tsao. It might be wishful thinking on my part, but it wasn't that wishful; I was very sure that when it came to dealing with the help, Tsao had done all the talking. Maybe, just once, I could turn Jewel's bizarre attempt to move into my life to my own advantage.

I got out my compact, flipped open the mirror, and tried to remember the makeup Jewel had been wearing this morning. I put on big bronze bars of eye shadow and enough black eyeliner to get a middle schooler grounded. Obviously, I couldn't conjure up a Versace dress—but then, it was perfectly believable that Jewel would have changed out of that during the middle of the day. She had done me a favor by matching my hair color; with a few bobby pins I put it up in a very acceptable copy of the style she had been wearing earlier today.

I looked at myself in my compact mirror. Not a bad copy of Jewel at all. I still wanted a little more to work with, though. I didn't have a key to the penthouse suite. To make the hotel staff break their own security regulations, I was going to have to be more than just a Disgruntled Guest.

Then an idea hit me. I had worked in a customer service industry, after all. I knew the one thing the hotel staff would fear more than a Disgruntled Guest: a disgruntled guest who was also a Secret Shopper. I felt my mouth curve slowly into a smile. Then I grabbed my purse, with the sketchbook on top, and headed back down to the lobby.

"Excuse me," I said to concierge. "Where could I find a restroom?" When I got the directions I grunted instead of saying thank you, careful not to smile. I walked off a couple of steps, making sure I was still well within the concierge's field of view, and then I took out my little notebook and scribbled a short comment.

When I snapped the notebook shut, the concierge was still watching me. *Good.* He smiled. I didn't.

I was looking for mistakes that I could complain about so the hotel staff would desperately want to please me, but unfortunately for Secret Shopper Girl, the bathroom was immaculate. The floor tiles were dazzlingly clean and white, there was no graffiti scratched into the bathroom stalls, and instead of cheap soap dispensers there were little racks of Hiram & Welker's Individually Wrapped Lavender Soap Bars stacked up like so many pats of butter next to the sink. Instead of paper towels, the hotel supplied linen washcloths which you were supposed to drop in a laundry basket after use. Environmentally friendly and classy as hell. I considered taking a couple of the washcloths and using them to stop up a toilet and create a small flood, as I had done once before when I needed to create a diversion, but that would just create a mess. Mess alone wasn't what I needed. I needed guilt.

I left the bathroom, turned left, and went down a short flight of stairs toward what the signs informed me was The Terrace Café. Just outside the café, the Montgomery Arms had installed a table with complimentary beverages—tea and coffee for the clientele. Or, strictly speaking, tea and caffeinated coffee. They hadn't put out a pot of decaf.

Hallelujah, I thought, blessing whatever poor soul had forgotten to refill the pot. *O Spirit of the Secret Shopper, be with me now.*

A couple walked past me. The hostess for The Terrace Café greeted them and took them to be seated. The moment

186.

her back was turned, I rifled through the basket of tea bags, scooping up all the English Breakfast, Irish Breakfast, and Earl Grey, leaving only Chamomile Dreams, Rosehip Refreshment, and Ginger Peach Zinger teas behind. I walked briskly back to the bathroom, dumped the extra tea bags into the laundry basket, and grabbed a couple of washcloths to cover them with. My eye fell on the individually wrapped bars of soap and I grabbed a gleeful handful.

I paused on the landing, extracting two small bars of soap from their wrappers, until I heard the Terrace Café hostess greet a group of German businessmen and say, "Right this way, gentlemen." Then I trotted quickly to the beverage table, lifted the top off the coffee urn, and dropped in the bars of soap with two small, satisfying *plops*.

Then it was back to the lobby. Walking with my notebook open in my hand I approached the concierge. The moment he saw me I flipped the notebook shut and stuck it in my purse, as if trying to hide it. "Excuse me," I said. "I'm afraid I have a problem."

The concierge jumped out from behind his desk with gratifying speed. "I'm very sorry to hear that. Perhaps I can help?"

I led him to the beverage table. "I don't mean to be a bother," I said, not smiling, "but you do announce a complimentary beverage service, don't you?"

"As you see," he said politely.

"I prefer not to drink caffeine after breakfast, but there isn't any decaffeinated coffee."

"Ah. Yes," he said. "Sometimes after the first pot is empty we don't make a second. Fewer people drink it, and it can get stale."

"I drink it," I said.

"I would be very happy to get you a cup from the café free of charge. Bev?" he said, signaling the hostess. "Could I get a cup of decaf here?"

"Thank you," I said. And flipping open my notebook I scribbled "no decaf." "Just bill it to our room. The penthouse suite."

"No charge," the concierge said graciously. "Please take it with the compliments of the house."

I tucked the notebook back in my purse. "When I couldn't get coffee, I looked for tea. But all you seem to have here are … hippie beverages. Rose ginger ginseng infusion, and so forth. I would just like plain black tea: orange pekoe, English breakfast, anything. That really didn't seem like too much to expect."

"That is unfortunate," the concierge said, "although I would have thought you would have preferred one of the herbal teas, since regular tea is caffeinated, while all of these," he said, fingering through the packets in the basket, "appear to be caffeine free."

Oops. "Just because it's decaf doesn't mean I want to drink it," I blustered. I held up a packet of Ginger Peach Zinger. "I realize this is San Francisco, but is there a memo I didn't see? Regular tea isn't cool enough to make the list? I mean, the kind with actual tea leaves in it?"

We made eye contact.

"I am *so* sorry," the concierge said. "Bev will see to it at once. Is there anything else?" He asked politely, as if he had all the time in the world and nothing better to do than listen to my complaints.

Damn, he was good.

For the first time, I let my expression soften. "You've been very patient with me, and I hate to make a fuss, but would you mind trying the coffee?"

"The caffeinated coffee?"

"I was desperate."

He gave a professional smile. "I know the feeling." He poured himself a cup of coffee. He sipped, and then, for the first time, his bulletproof poise slipped and his eyes bugged out. Hiram & Welker's Individually Wrapped Lavender Soap Bars had done their work. He put the cup down. "This coffee is completely unacceptable. Bev," he called, in a distinctly sharper voice. The hostess trotted over with my cup of decaf. "You need to replace the coffee at once. Use a new urn and wash this one out. And if Ernesto has been up to his tricks again, he can consider himself unemployed." Bev looked alarmed and jumped to obey.

I took out my notebook and made another little annotation.

"Please, let me assure you that this is not a typical experience at The Montgomery Arms. Is there anything else I can do for you?" the concierge said anxiously as we returned to the lobby. "Tickets to a show tonight, or perhaps a Giants game? We keep a few complimentary passes for our preferred guests. Or perhaps you would like a complimentary dinner at the restaurant tonight?"

Instead of answering, I fished in my purse. "Well, damn," I said. "I left my room key in my other bag." Our eyes met. I could see the concierge calculating risks and rewards. I was amazed he could hear himself think over the hammering of my heart.

"But of course," he said, after the briefest of hesitations, and

189.

he escorted me to the reception desk. "Monica? Could you please issue another card for Ms…?"

Yikes! What name would Jewel have used? No, wait— Jewel didn't matter. "Tsao's suite," I said. "Tsao Kuo Ch'iu."

Monica smiled. "Of course," she said.

Perfume (Hour of the Engagement Present)

Three minutes later I was standing in front of Tsao's door. I knocked, just to make sure Tsao and Jewel hadn't gotten back yet. I was all ready to say, "Housekeeping! We'll come back later!" in a Jamaican accent if anyone answered, but nobody did. I stood on the threshold while my heart pounded once, twice, five times, ten. *Enough already, Cathy. Do it.* I slid the card key into the lock, opened the door, and stepped quickly inside, closing the door behind myself.

The first thing that struck me about the penthouse suite was the spectacular view. There was a huge picture window across from me, framing the whole bay, so I could see the Golden Gate Bridge, Alcatraz, and Angel Island behind it. There was a sliding glass door at one end of the room leading to a balcony. Standing out there at sunset with Victor on my arm would make the incredibly pricey room seem almost worth it.

The second thing I noticed was the smell of Jewel's peach-scented perfume. The room was saturated with the stuff, and the effect in a closed space wasn't entirely pleasant. In the mall I had assumed Tsao had treated her to something truly upscale, but the heavy odor that clung to the suite's elegant upholstery had an unpleasant, slightly medical undertone—camphor, or formaldehyde.

190.

The third thing I noticed was Tsao, so I forgot about those first two things in a hurry. He was coming out of the bathroom with his face newly washed and his hair slicked back. Obviously Jewel, if she was around, was in the back bedroom and expecting him to answer the door, but he hadn't heard my knock because the tap was running. Water droplets dripped off his fingers.

We stared at one another.

I jumped for the door.

Too late. Before I could get back into the corridor he had me by the arm and was guiding me inexorably back inside. "Cathy! Please come in. Have a seat," he said, pointing to the couch.

"Uh, that's okay. I think I'll stand."

"As you like." The door closed with a click, locking me into the room with Tsao. He looked at me with a mix of hunger and skepticism that was not reassuring. "I don't suppose you have reconsidered my offer?"

"Well, yes, actually. I have a quick temper," I said apologetically. "I decided I should at least hear what you had to say without flying off the handle."

"I don't believe you." Tsao smiled. "I think you came looking to steal your scarf."

"Also possible," I admitted.

Jewel appeared in the doorway to the bedroom, still wearing the Versace. "Who . . . Oh. It's you." She cocked her head to one side. "You put your hair up. I get it—you pretended to be me to get a room key, right?"

"Don't flatter yourself." Tsao didn't bother to look at her. "You are the copy, my dear. Cathy will always be the original."

"Call the cops," I told Jewel. "Tell them he killed Auntie Joe. He can't catch us both."

191.

Jewel sized up the situation. "Yeah, I wonder which one of us is closer to the door," she said sarcastically. "I don't feel like getting my neck broken so you can make a break for it. As for you," Jewel said, glancing at Tsao, "you could be at least a little nice to me."

"This can still work out," Tsao said earnestly to me. "I kept Jewel around for a reason, Cathy. The scarf has your fingerprints on it, true, but it also has hers. If I give Jewel to the police, the whole thing goes away."

"You're crazy," I said.

"I'm in love," Tsao said. "A related phenomenon, I assure you."

"It's not that easy," I said. "Jewel will tell her side of the story. She'll drag me into it, and you, and everyone else she can."

"Jesus H. Christ, Cathy, you're so *stupid,*" Jewel said, fishing in her Gucci handbag. "Tsao isn't going to turn me over to the cops *alive*. Right? He's gonna smother me and claim it was heart failure. Or, no, drugs is better. A drug overdose and the hotel staff finds me in the bathtub. How am I doing?" she asked Tsao. "Am I close?"

"I was thinking of the balcony," Tsao said, still looking only at me. "It's thirteen floors down, Cathy. One push and we solve two problems, Auntie Joe's death and the continuing existence of your cheap imitation here." He smiled. "Consider it an engagement present."

I looked at him, horrified.

"Ah," Jewel said. "Found it." She pulled a gun out of her Gucci handbag. She dropped the handbag on the couch so she could get a steady two-handed grip on the gun and pointed it at

192.

Tsao. "You should have been a little nicer to me."

"Go ahead," Tsao said. "It won't—"

Jewel pulled the trigger. The blast was deafening. There was a hole in the middle of Tsao's chest and a fat splatter of blood appeared on the wall behind him. Blood bubbled down the front of his shirt like water coming from a broken hose. Tsao looked down, puzzled. He dabbed at the blood with his fingers. It kept coming and coming.

"Time to find out how the other half lives," Jewel said. The gun was rock steady in her two-handed grip.

"Oh, my god," I whispered. "The perfume!"

Tsao turned his head to look at me, still confused. He was swaying on his feet, his balance starting to go.

I stared at Jewel, wide-eyed. "*You're* the one who had the mortality serum. Victor said Lu found a way to make it an aerosol. You've been wearing a cloud of it for days. That's how Auntie Joe got exposed. And that's why Tsao started acting so weird, losing his temper. He was human again, even though he didn't know it."

"You do notice things," Jewel said. "That's something I admire about you."

Tsao crumpled to his knees. "Cathy?" he said. "I will l-love you…" Blood seeped out of his mouth. "I will love you *forever*."

Jewel walked toward Tsao. She stopped just out of arm's reach and pointed the gun at his head. "One other thing," she said. "Nobody hits my brother but me, you son of a bitch."

I turned away just before the second shot.

193.

First Time for Everything

Jewel and I stood there looking at the body. My ears were ringing. A charred firecracker smell rose into the air that was already thick with the stink of blood and peach-scented perfume. "Whoa," Jewel said, lowering the gun. "I never did that before." She ran into the bathroom to throw up, but she took the gun with her. She came back a minute later, wiping her mouth. "Okay," she said. "Now I guess we gotta think what to do."

"He was going to kill you," I said. "I'll tell the cops it was self-defense."

"Thanks, but no thanks." Jewel knelt down beside Tsao's body and started going through his pockets. "I knew this guy once, he had some tats and he was big, right, so he got a job as a bouncer at this club, you know? So one night this famous basketball player comes into the bar and drinks 'til they have to cut him off and this friend of mine's supposed to throw him out, which he does, and then the guy's posse comes back an hour later and shoots him in the neck. I get there right when the cops are wrapping it up and I hear them talking. Fat cop says to thin cop, 'File it under NHI.'" Jewel found Tsao's wallet and opened it up. "You know what NHI stands for?" I shook my head. "It's for bag ladies and dealers and whores. It means, 'no human involved.' That was my friend. Fat, you know, and tattoos. NHI." She pulled all the cash out of Tsao's wallet without even looking up at me. "People like me, we're disposable."

"What are you going to do?"

"I dunno." She stood up and her eyes wandered back to Tsao, lying on the blood-soaked carpet. "Jesus. I never did that before."

194.

"I won't turn you in," I said.

"I don't believe you." Jewel looked around the penthouse suite. "I've got a million prints here anyway, and the staff has seen me. I could shoot you, but I don't think it would help much."

"Me neither."

"It's not really a vote." Abruptly Jewel swung the gun around to point it at me. "Give me your driver's license."

"What? I can't—" She twitched the gun and I shut my mouth. I pulled my wallet out of my purse, took out my driver's license and handed it over.

She studied the picture on the front. "I think I could pass for you, if they don't look at the picture real hard…"

"What are you going to do about the gun?"

"It was his. Not sure," she said, frowning. "I guess I'll stick it in the bag for now and ditch it later."

"How did you get the serum?"

"You know, much as I'd love to sit around and be girlfriends, I figure somebody heard the shots, so I'm going to skedaddle and save the storytelling for some other time," Jewel said. "You stay here for sixty seconds, and then do whatever you like." She stuffed the gun into her purse and headed for the door. She put her hand on the knob and turned around. "Cathy?"

"Yeah?"

"I really am sorry about your dad," she said.

195.

An Unexpected Party (Hour of the Slightly Tardy Rescue Attempt)

Sixty seconds later the door to the penthouse suite smashed open and Victor charged inside. "Cathy!" I waved. He stopped in his tracks, staring at the mutilated corpse of Tsao Kuo Ch'iu lying on the floor.

"Oh, my god, Victor," I said. "Your father . . ."

"He was no father to me," Victor said flatly, but I could see that he was shaken.

Emma and Pete appeared in the doorway, gasping. "Cathy!" Emma panted. "We came to rescue you!"

"Thanks," I said, and I meant it.

"Whoa." Pete took in the body. "Uh, Emma—I don't think you want to look at this." Emma nodded, white-faced.

Victor looked from Tsao's corpse back to me. "I guess our rescuing came a little late."

"It's the thought that counts," I said. "As it happens, Jewel rescued me first." The three of them stared back at me, dumbfounded, but what had happened between my double and I felt too recent and too private to explain. "So how did you track me down?"

"As soon as I realized you'd given me the slip back at the hospital, I called Emma. She guessed you might be coming here." Victor headed into Tsao's bedroom and started searching through the drawers. His eye fell on Tsao's briefcase. He grabbed it, popped the latches, and made a small pleased noise. He lifted out the white silk scarf he had given me a few months before. "I think this belongs to you."

I balled it up and stuffed it into my purse.

"We should get going," Emma said. "Pete's truck is right

196.

downstairs. I was so worried we valet parked."

"Wow!" I said, genuinely astonished.

"Didn't want to lose my best friend," Emma said. My eyes were getting shiny with gratitude as I looked at the three of them.

"Move now, cry later," Victor said. He poked his head out of the door. "All clear. Head for the stairs."

We jogged quickly after him. "Hey—I *know* the stairway door was locked," I said. "How did you guys get past that?"

Victor turned and grinned over his shoulder at me. "That was Pete," he said. "You'll see."

I turned the corner of the corridor and there at the end of the hallway under the EXIT sign was an empty doorway. The tall metal door was leaning neatly against the wall beside it. Pete grinned and held up a Swiss Army knife with the Phillips screwdriver attachment out. "It doesn't matter how good the lock on the door is if you can just unscrew the hinges that hold it to the wall."

I laughed. "Wow. Smart."

"Eye for personnel," Emma gasped as she caught up. "Number one requirement in a chief executive. Now *keep running!*"

Then we were flying down the stairs three or four at a time, huge clattering steps that threw up a thunder of echoes in the concrete stairwell. When we got all the way down to the ground floor, I cracked the stairway door and peered out just in time to see the concierge loping to the elevators behind a hysterical maid. As soon as the elevator doors slid closed behind him we headed out into the lobby, trying not to run or do anything suspicious. Pete fished out his valet ticket while Victor gave him money to cover parking and a tip.

197.

Five minutes later we were on the 280, headed for home. Victor was looking through the oddments he'd grabbed from Tsao's briefcase. "Did you get anything else?" he asked me.

"Just this," I said, opening my purse and taking out a small cut glass bottle.

"It looks like perfume," Emma said curiously.

"I got it out of Jewel's purse when she went into the bathroom to throw up."

Victor looked at me, puzzled. "Why would you want that?"

I don't know why I didn't explain what was in the bottle. Maybe because it felt private, something personal between Jewel and me. And maybe—I'm not proud of this—maybe there was something in me that wanted, just once, to know something even the mighty immortals didn't know. To have a way of hurting them, if you want the ugliest version. That's what Jewel had done. For the first time in history, one of Them had tried to abandon a poor, weak, fragile, worthless one of Us: and been denied.

"Oh, I don't know," I said. "I guess I just wanted something to remember her by."

Pancakes (Hour of My Mother)

I got Pete to drop me off at home and told everyone I would meet them at the hospital in a couple of hours. It was just four o'clock.

When I stepped up onto the porch I found a small padded envelope leaning against our front door with nothing on it but my name. I tore it open. Inside was a small painting, beautifully framed. It was a family portrait, me and Mom and Dad.   Mom was relaxed and she was smiling at Dad the way she did when she teased him.   My hair was being good for once, glimmering with the little red highlights I got in summer sometimes.   My father's dark eyes didn't look sad at all, but crinkled at the edges.   We were so happy in that picture. Happier than we were in real life, maybe.

There was a note.

Here's a quick something I knocked out after your memorable departure from Cohn this morning. If you think it might help your mom, tell her you found it in my study. Maybe it will give her something to remember. For your own part, it's probably best to forget.

—Dad

199.

I would have said I couldn't cry anymore, but something twisted my heart like a rag, wringing out more tears.

I touched the paint. It was dry. Another shock went through me, tender and painful, as if someone had pressed on a bruise that went down to the very core of my body. Maybe everything my father had said at the funeral was true. Maybe my mother was one woman out of dozens he had known. Maybe I was one child out of hundreds. But this wasn't something he had whipped up since the funeral as a peace offering to me. This was a portrait he had worked on, carefully, tenderly, patiently, over days or maybe weeks in the bleak months since he abandoned us. "Liar," I whispered. He wanted me to think he didn't love us . . . but the paint was dry.

I let myself into the house. I stashed the painting in my room and stood over the bathroom sink until the tears finally stopped coming. I heard my mom's alarm go off as I finished washing my face and I decided to make her breakfast. Pancakes. I went into the kitchen. For some reason Mom and I never ate in the dining room anymore. It seemed too empty for just the two of us. Mom and I didn't share a whole lot of meals these days, but when we did, we ate them at the kitchen table.

My dad taught me to make pancakes from scratch; he thought buying pancake mix from the supermarket was the dumbest thing ever. I grabbed a mixing bowl from under the shelf and put in a cup of flour, a teaspoon of baking powder and a pinch of salt. I got a whisk and mixed the dry ingredients together. Mom shambled into the bathroom and I could hear the tap running. I put in a dollop of oil, one egg, and enough milk to make the batter the right consistency. Whisk, whisk,

200.

whisk. I put in a capful of vanilla, too, and two capfuls of orange extract and some extra sugar. Orange pancakes. He used to make her that on her birthdays.

Mom padded into the kitchen, belting up her dressing gown. "Hey, kiddo," she said, yawning. "Whatcha makin'?"

"Orange pancakes."

She blinked. "What's the occasion?"

"No occasion," I said. "Just thought you might like something for breakfast."

"At four in the afternoon?"

"It's breakfast for you."

"True." She filled up the coffeemaker and turned it on while I finished mixing my batter. I grabbed the griddle and put it on the stove. When I figured it'd had time to get hot I wet my fingers in the sink and then flicked the water onto the skillet. The droplets sizzled and spat. Hot enough.

The coffeemaker chortled happily to itself and began to perk. The smell of fresh coffee crept into the kitchen. "This is nice," Mom said warily. "Did you get in an accident with the car?"

"Mom!"

"Just asking."

"No, I did not trash the car." I grabbed a ladle from the Big Implement Drawer and ladled out four spoonfuls of batter, one in each corner of the griddle. "How was your day?" I asked. "Well, night, I guess."

"Cathy?" my mother said sharply. "Are you pregnant?"

"Mom!"

"Well, what is it, then? Why are you acting so different?"

"Don't you like it?"

"Sure I like it." She grabbed the coffee pot and poured

201.

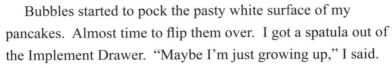

herself a cup. It smelled good. "I just want to know what's causing it."

Bubbles started to pock the pasty white surface of my pancakes. Almost time to flip them over. I got a spatula out of the Implement Drawer. "Maybe I'm just growing up," I said.

My mother laughed at that, which was what was supposed to happen. She asked if I wanted some coffee and I said yes. She poured me a cup, to which I added three spoons of sugar and lots of cream. My mom is a black-no-sugar woman, but I basically believe in turning my coffee into cheesecake.

I remembered about syrup just as I was flipping the pancakes. I grabbed some orange juice out of the fridge and put it in a saucepan to simmer with two tablespoons of brown sugar. "So, you were going to tell me about your day, Mom."

"It wasn't so great." My mother sipped her coffee. "There was a guy in last night, forty-four years old, massive ischemic event." I looked over. "Stroke," she said. "Paralyzed one side of his face. No speech. Hard to tell how much brain damage there is. Sometimes they're vegetables, but sometimes they stay smart, you know, totally aware, only they just can't talk. Your uncle Stanley was like that. Ten years of being trapped inside his own head—smart as a tack but couldn't say a word. Had to be helped to the bathroom, everything. God, I would hate that worse than anything," she said. "I don't ever want to be a burden."

I slid the pancakes onto a plate for her and put them on the table along with a knife and fork and the saucepan with the orange syrup. "Thanks," she said. I could still hear the surprise in her voice. I ladled out the rest of the batter. I didn't feel hungry, but if you don't cook the batter right away it ends up getting covered in plastic wrap and shoved into the fridge, where it drifts slowly but inexorably to the back and develops colonies of mold that eventually grow larger and more intricate, developing agriculture and primitive writing systems, or even, if you don't clean your fridge very often, inventing talk radio and The Shopping Channel.

Really, it's best to cook the batter right away and nip that in the bud.

My mom frowned into her cup of coffee. "His poor wife was there, and two kids. The daughter was the one who found him. She kept explaining that she didn't know what was wrong at first. As if she was worried the stroke wouldn't have been so bad if she had done something faster. Which might be true." Mom took another swallow of black coffee. "Poor kid." She buttered her pancakes and poured syrup over them and took a bite.

"How are they?"

"Good!" she said, forgetting not to talk when her mouth was full. "Really good, Cathy." I kept my eye on the griddle, waiting for bubbles to show in the second set of pancakes. "Anyway, the whole scene just reminded me of you, you know." She looked down at her plate. "Of what happened to us. I felt so bad about being in Mexico, kid. I can't imagine how horrible it must have been for you to find your father. I should have been there."

Coffee burbled into the coffeemaker. On the griddle, my pancakes hissed. I turned them over. "I can't believe you do that job every day," I said.

"You know, I give you all kinds of crap," my mom said, "but the truth is, you've had it way harder than I ever did, kiddo. My parents made a better life for me than we ever did for you." Her eyes were shiny. That didn't happen very often. "You know, the first year after your father died, I kept thinking, I'm a nurse, for Christ's sake! I should have seen it coming. I should have noticed something."

You should have noticed he wasn't getting older, I thought to myself. *You should have wondered why he encouraged you to take that weekend in Mexico. You should have told me your contact numbers instead of trusting him to do it. But as tough as you are, as cynical as you can be, Mom, you never imagined betrayal on that scale.* Out loud I said, "There was nothing you could do."

She shrugged.

I put the second batch of pancakes on another plate and turned the heat off under the griddle. I grabbed a knife and fork for myself and spread butter on my pancakes. Well, not really butter, we can't afford that. It's actually some kind of canola oil spread, but I prefer to think of it as butter.

I kept thinking I was going to tell my mother the truth about my dad, but the moment kept slipping away and apparently I was just going to eat pancakes instead. It felt like the right thing to do at the time. It felt like the right choice.

"Yeah, I don't beat myself up so much anymore." My mother looked down at her coffee cup, then back at me. "Now I just wish I had been kinder."

Our eyes met. Sitting with her plate of half-eaten pancakes in front of her she looked young. Vulnerable. That was always true with my mom—never would take crap from anybody, but kindness just unstrung her. "Listen," I said, "I was up in the studio the other day, and I found something I think you should see…"

Forever (Hour of What Comes Next?)

I told Mom I wanted to visit a friend in the hospital and asked if I could catch a ride with her when she drove into work. "Today will be better," she said as we pulled into the parking lot. "I'm starting a rotation in obstetrics. Labor isn't fun, but mostly people are happy in obstetrics."

"And sore," I said.

"Sore, but happy. That's kids for ya."

We parked and I went up to see Denny. As Victor had promised, Denny was thoroughly tanked on painkillers, drifting peacefully in and out of consciousness. Pete, Emma, and Victor were already there when I arrived. Emma had brought flowers for Denny, although frankly a can of motor oil or a six-pack of beer probably would have been more appropriate. By the time I arrived, Emma was diagramming a design for the Cathy's Key website on the back of one of Denny's medical charts. Pete was absentmindedly starting to disassemble the hospital bed controls, although he sheepishly put them back together when I caught him at it.

205.

206.

The hospital had that hospital smell: bleach and laundry, sick people, formaldehyde and dying flowers.

Victor gave Emma and Pete forty bucks and sent them out in search of something for us to eat. I checked the Blackberry and found that it was dead. "Hunh. Chad finally got around to getting his line disconnected."

"Which you should do with your phone," Victor said, wincing. "Just to make my life a little less confusing. Please?"

"I don't know. . . . At least as long as Jewel has my phone, I have some way to get in touch with her."

"Why would you want to?"

I shrugged. "We're not . . . done with one another yet, I don't think. Did I mention that she is out there in the world somewhere with my driver's license?"

Victor looked like he'd just sucked on a lemon. "Oh, man. Where do you think she is right now?"

"On a bus, I bet." Sitting at the back of some trolley groaning its way up Mission street, or maybe tucked into the dim interior of a Greyhound headed to God knows where.

"What a disaster," Victor said.

"Maybe. But she was more than a match for Tsao, you know."

"I wonder what happened to him?" Victor said. "Obviously Lu got the mortality serum into him somehow."

I didn't tell him about the perfume then, either. "So what about you?" I said. "What's next?"

"You," Victor said with a tired smile. "I burned all my bridges with Lu Yan at the service today. Don't kid yourself; we've just made a very powerful enemy, you and I."

"You mean, you're thinking of actually sticking around with me?" I said. "I'm amazed. Haven't you been trying to get away from me for the last six months?"

"Totally true." He stepped over to the window, looking out over the hospital parking lot. "But nothing seems to work."

He seemed to tense for an instant. "Problem?" I said.

"Hm? Oh, no. I just saw… I just remembered something I saw at the gift shop," he said. "Hang on a sec. I'll be right back."

While he was gone I looked at Denny, lying pale and broken and drugged in his hospital bed, and thought about what fragile creatures people are, and thought about Jewel. She must have been in touch with Ancestor Lu, must have cut a deal with him that Tsao didn't know about. He had made a big mistake, thinking she was just a cheap amusement he could use as a bargaining chip with me. Whatever else she was, Jewel was a survivor.

When you're mortal, sometimes that's the only thing that matters.

"I have a present for you," Victor said when he returned. He held out both fists. "Guess which hand?" There was a scrape on his left knuckle so I picked that one. "Good guess," he said. He opened his hand. Lying in his palm was a Chinese coin, one of those ones with a hole in the middle, along with a silk cord to hang it from. "You can wear it like a necklace. It's supposed to be good luck."

"I thought you didn't know anything about Chinese folklore."

He grinned, threading the coin on the silk cord. "That's what the lady in the gift shop said." He turned me around and put the necklace on me. The coin brushed a little below my throat. I could feel the warmth of his fingers on the back of my neck as he tied the cord and then turned me gently around so we were face to face once more. He looked at me. "Actually, I think I must be the lucky one," he said, and we kissed.

We kissed, and time stopped and it was perfect and it was

forever: but when the kiss ended I pulled back, and I was crying.

"Hey, now," Victor said. Gently, gently. He reached up with one knuckle and pulled a tear down my cheek. It glistened on his beautiful hand.

"Do you think it's true, what my dad said? That we can't ever be together?" I looked down at Denny, zoned on painkillers, one poor arm in a cast and the other one with a giant IV needle taped inside his elbow. "The last thing Tsao told me was that he would love me forever. But love isn't forever, you know?" Victor tried to take my hand, but I pulled it away. "The whole point of love is that it happens now. Here. Between daybreak and nightfall."

Victor said, "Not all men are like your dad, Cathy."

"No," I said. "But you are."

Silence.

"I love you," I said. "At least, I think I do. I did. But what about Giselle, Victor? What about Bianca? What about the sister you left behind, and the son, and the daughter, and the wife. Wives."

"I can change."

"Can you?" I looked at him. "Should you? I don't know. And I don't think you know, either."

Victor was very still. "So what are you saying, Cathy?"

"I don't know."

"I do," Denny croaked.

Victor and I turned around, startled. Denny cracked open one drug-hazed eye. His speech was slurred, and his eyeballs had a disturbing habit of rolling up into his head. "It's ver' simple, Kung Fu," he said deliberately. "That chick is *into* me." Denny's eyeballs did the gross disappearing thing again.

"Yup. She's feeling the pull of the LOVE muzzle," he said. "Muscle, I mean."

"Uh, Denny," I said.

"We got lots in common." Denny added a dignified hiccup.

"Such as?"

"Oh, you know. *Stuff.*" He tried to wink at me, but it sort of slurred into a leer. Then his eyes rolled up in his head again.

"I think he passed out," Victor said.

Denny gurgled. "You wish." With great effort, he managed to get both eyes open and focused at the same time. "Don' take it hard, bro. Chick's jus' tryin to let you down easy."

For some reason I was blushing furiously. "I never said that!"

"Cathy an' Denny/ Sittin' in a tree/ K-I-S-S-M-P-G..." he burbled. "You may be a *fighta*, Kung Fu, but you ain't no LOVAH!"

Victor was looking at me with a curious glint in his eye. "Fair enough," he said. "Me against the mortals. Forever against a day. And may the best man—"

"Szzngmp," Denny snored.

And we laughed.

209.

Fiction (Hour of Emma's Cunning Plan™)

"You're gonna love this," Pete said enthusiastically as
he trotted into Denny's hospital room with two pizza boxes,
an extra-large and a mini size. He dumped the mini on the
window ledge and reverently opened the lid on the extra-
large. Steam rolled out, carrying the unmistakable smell of
fish. "It's called the Salty Dog—goat cheese, pineapple, olives,
and anchovies! There's only one place that makes them in the
whole Bay Area!"

"Imagine that," I said. "What's in the other box?"

"That's just a pepperoni, in case Victor likes bland food,"
Emma said. With a sinking feeling I remembered that Emma
had grown up in Hong Kong eating cuttlefish and salted plums;
I had no doubt she would think an olive and anchovy pizza
was a great idea. Victor and I made a grab for the pepperoni
mini-box. His reflexes were faster but I wanted it more and he
backed slowly away from the glare in my eyes.

"The thing I worry about," Emma said, chomping happily
through her first slice of Salty Dog, "is that Jewel is still out there
with your diary. God knows what she'll try to do with it next."

Victor eyed the pepperoni meekly. Relenting, I gave him
one slice. "Ancestor Lu won't like that," he said. "He doesn't
like leaving loose ends."

Victor and I were sitting in the room's two chairs while
Emma perched on the windowsill. Pete settled on the edge
of Denny's bed and began stuffing himself with pizza. "We
could try to trace her cell phone. I can't do that hack, but I
know some guys who might be able to," he offered through a
mouthful of cheese.

Denny swam briefly back into consciousness. "God

almighty, what is that smell?"

"Goat cheese, pineapple, olives, and anchovies!" Pete and Emma chorused happily. Denny's eyes rolled back into his head.

Emma suddenly stopped in mid-chew. "Wait!"

Pete poked Denny doubtfully in the side. "I think he passed out again."

"No, don't worry about him. It's about the diary. I have a plan," Emma announced. "We've been thinking about this all wrong. We want to get it back, hide it, lay low. That's how Ancestor Lu would do it. But what we should do is the exact opposite." She looked around at the ring of confused faces. "We should *publish* it."

"What?" I said, speaking for all of us.

"Publish it! Pretend it's just a story," Emma said. "Then nobody will take it seriously!"

"Publish my diary?"

"Publish everything! The diary, the newspaper clippings, the birth certificates—everything! Then, even though there's tons of evidence about the immortals right out there in the real world, *it will all seem like fiction,*" Emma said happily. "Nobody cares about fiction." She gulped down the last bite of her piece of pizza. "Turning it into a story hides the truth about the immortals more effectively than Ancestor Lu could ever do." She licked her fingers and helped herself to a second slice. "Besides, this way we could make a little money on it." She looked up and found us all staring at her, transfixed. She looked down, checking her shirt for pizza stains. "What?"

"Emma," I breathed, "you are a genius!"

THE END.

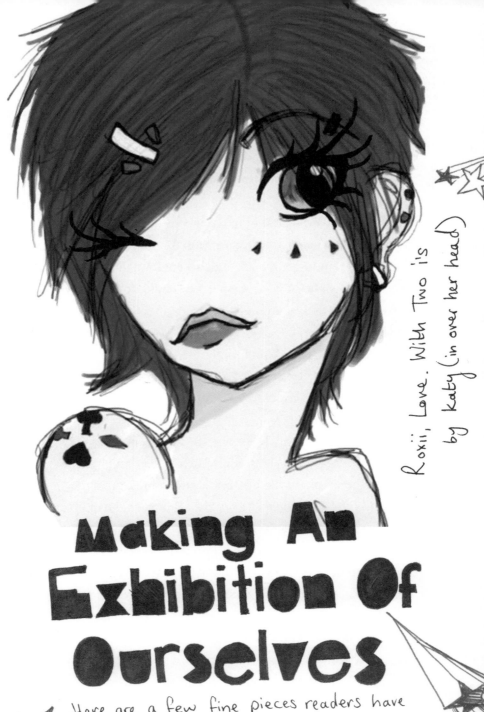

Roxii, Love. With Two i's
by katy (in over her head)

Making An Exhibition Of Ourselves

Here are a few fine pieces readers have submitted to A Prestigious Gallery, our shared artspace at www.cathyskey.com Check it out!

My Life on a Page
by Katie Hughes

Cry me a River
by Sarah O'Neill

Tempestuous Butterfly
by Jisell

sarah

Baki Man
by Rebecca A.

The Number You Have Dialed...
(Hour of the Disconnected Phone)

Phone numbers disconnected ✉

Send Now | 🗎 📎 🗇 🗑 🖨 Print ▾ | Insert ▾ | 🗃 ▾ 📋 Categories ▾ 📁 Projects ▾

To: 📧 *private@cathyskey.com*
Cc:

Subject: Phone numbers disconnected

▶ Attachments: *none*

Verdana ▾ | 14 ▾ | **B** *I* U T | ☰ ☰ ☰ | ⅓⅔ ⅓⅔ ⟨⟨ ⟩⟩ | ▴A ▾ ◆ ▾ —

Hey Cathy—

Just doing a routine check, I noticed Bianca had disconnected her number and it looks like some messages have been deleted, too.

Can you test the archive? Go to <u>www.doubletalkwireless.com</u>

Is that girl smart or what !!!

"Check Messages"

Try putting in Bianca's number: 510-286-7995. You should hear her answering machine message.

Then, if you put in her password (1111), you can hear the message Victor left for her. ◄

(The password is her birthday, BTW – November 11. Remember V mumbled something about it being a special day?)

Your personal bug Tester,

E

Carla's Office :
408-236 – 3715

Carla's Home # is on the daytimer page in Cathy's Book !
(access code 1493)

Victor... erased message at access code 5555 (where'd that come from?)

Just listened to message on Emma's phone at code 3030 whoa !!!

Cathy & Victor's story continues in

Cathy's Ring

If found call (650) 266 - 8263

Turn the page to read ▶ the first exciting Chapter!

Turn the page to read ▶ the first exciting Chapter!

And visit:
www. cathysring .com

Pot of Poison (Hour of my Evil Twin)

Mom was at the hospital working the graveyard shift and I was alone in the sweltering house. I had turned off the air conditioning as soon as she left for work, trying to save money. On hot nights like this, going to bed felt like I was pitching a tent in a toaster over, but in view of my spectacular failure to pay my share of the mortgage it seemed like the least I could do. Summer was getting on and it had been months since the dust had tasted rain. Wildfire season had started: a twenty thousand acre blaze in the Sierra foothills, and closer to home big grass fires were burning near Gilroy and Vacaville and Palo Alto. Dozens of smaller fires had left patches of blackened grass along the freeways all the way into San Francisco.

I changed into my lightest PJs but after a second I decided not to take off the good luck charm my boyfriend, Victor, had given me—the Chinese coin threaded on a slim silver chain—that he said he picked up at the hospital gift shop earlier in the day. The unfamiliar weight swung and bumped against my collar bone as I trudged into the bathroom to splash my face with cold water. The eyes looking back at me from the mirror were bloodshot and exhausted. I shambled back into my bedroom and opened the window wide. There was no breeze, just the smell of burning, as if someone in the distance was holding a match to the darkness and waiting for it to catch. I shoved the blankets off my bed and lay down on top of the sheets to wait for sleep. It had only been ten hours since I'd seen a man shot. Every time I closed my eyes I saw him looking at his bloody chest in surprise: saw the red blood soaking into the carpet and spattered on the wallpaper behind him. In the darkness the scorched air smelled like gunpowder.

1.

The dead man's name was Tsao. The last thing he said before he died was, "Cathy, I will love you forever."

They say love warms the soul, but it burns it sometimes, too.

It was after midnight when I gave up trying to sleep. I crawled out of bed, turned on the bedroom light and closed my window. I dug a perfume bottle out of my purse and sat on the end of my bed to examine it. The bottle was almost round, shaped like a piece of crystal fruit, an apple or a peach. The heavy stopper had been fashioned into a stem with one leaf still clinging to it. The liquid inside was the color of a quarter cup of sunlight with a teaspoon of blood mixed in.

I brought the bottle of perfume up close to my face and took out the stopper. I used to smell things by leaning in and sorta sucking air through my nose, like most people do, but when I was being trained as a perfume demonstrator at the mall they told me you actually get more fragrance if you breathe normally with your mouth a little open and waft the air towards you with your hand. I let the scent curl around me, a sweet odor like peaches with an ugly little undertone of formaldehyde and smoke. It smelled like desire without hope. Like angels burning.

My phone rang and I picked it up instantly, thinking it would be someone in trouble, Emma or Victor. I was half right.

"You stole my perfume," said an angry voice with a sharp Texas twang.

"Hey, it's my Evil Twin, Jewel." The last time we were in a room together, ten hours ago, she was the one who killed Tsao. Then she took the money out of his wallet and forced me to give her my driver's license at gunpoint. I had been hoping I would never hear from her again. This is known as wishful thinking. "Gee, it's great to hear your voice," I said. In the background I could hear drunk people talking, bottles clinking, and the steady thud-thud of loud obnoxious dance music. "Where are you calling from?"

"Payphone at the Baptist church," Jewel said. "Listen, you took that perfume out of my purse this afternoon."

"No way," I said, turning the crystal bottle in my hands. "That would be stealing." Strictly speaking, the liquid in the bottle wasn't really perfume, it was a very special sort of poison—a complex chemical agent that took away the gift of immortality. My life had suffered a sudden and surprising infestation of immortals—my father, my boyfriend, and my boyfriend's angry ex-boss, Ancestor Lu, to name but a few—so to tell you the truth, there was something very comforting about holding that little pot of poison. In a small, mean way it felt good to think that with one well-timed spritz those godlike beings with eternal lives, lightning reflexes, and supernatural healing abilities could be reduced to ordinary human status again, at the mercy of pain and time and death like the rest of us. "Maybe you just forgot where you put it," I said. "For example, I can't find my driver's license."

"Very funny." I could hear Jewel stop to take a drink of something. "Have the cops showed up yet?"

"Not yet." Ever since I got home I had been wondering if I was about to get a visit from the Flat Feet of the Law. Because of an incident a few months back, the police had my fingerprints on file. If they got a good print from the hotel room, it was only a matter of time until their computers would identify me as a person of interest in Tsao's murder. Technically speaking I was innocent, but lying to the police

3.

is always dangerous, and telling them the truth—that my boyfriend's immortal dad had a crush on me but was shot to death by my evil twin after having been dosed with a secret Mortality Serum—was obviously a non-starter.

Jewel turned her mouth away from the phone. "Barkeep," she said. "Hey, *Numb Nuts*—yeah, you. **Gimme another beer.** Okay, I'm back. No cops, huh? Well, that might be good, or it might be bad." She chugged thoughtfully on her beer. "Good version, maybe you just didn't leave a lot of prints."

"What's the bad version?"

"Well, Tsao told me Ancestor Lu has some real spooky computer guys who can make things like police records just disappear. They might have wiped out your old fingerprint files."

"Why would Ancestor Lu do me a favor?"

"He wouldn't," Jewel said drily. "The bad version is that Lu wants to take you out himself, and you're easier to whack if you aren't locked up in a nice secure jail cell."

I swallowed. "Ah."

"How's Denny?" Jewel asked. "Did you get him to a doctor?" Denny was Jewel's brother. Tsao had broken his arm earlier in the day. The last thing Jewel said before she killed Tsao was, "Nobody hits my brother but me."

"He's in the hospital. I was there until a couple of hours ago. He won't be playing the piano any time soon, but he'll live."

"Listen, Cathy, you got to get him to head back to Texas. If he don't get back, the you-know-what's gonna hit the fan with his probation officer."

4.

"Loyalty's a big thing with your brother, Jewel. He's not going to leave you here."

"I know it. That's why you're going to tell him you talked to me and I was already back home."

Rap music pounded and thumped from Jewel's end of the phone. "Calling from a church," I said.

"He can tell when I'm lying but he's sweet on you. He doesn't know any better."

"Jewel—"

"*Hey*," she said sharply. "You drug my brother into this mess, Cathy. You get him out. Do it first thing tomorrow," she added. "I want to make sure he gets the message before Ancestor Lu's people take you out." Then she hung up.

It took me quite a while to get to sleep.

Scissors (Hour of Someone Coming to Kill Me)

I woke up with a gasp, terrified, staring into the darkness of my bedroom. My heart was pounding and I was listening for something, awake and electric, as if my whole skin was waiting for a sound. The clock on my bedside table said 4:13 AM.

There!

I heard it again, something gnawing at my bedroom window. Someone was working around the frame with pliers or a screwdriver. Trying to get in. Someone was coming for me, just like Jewel had said they would.

I needed help. I was alone in the darkness and nobody would hear me scream. Ever since my Dad "died" there had only been two of us

5.

in the house, my mom and me, and my mom was at the hospital working the graveyard shift. My cell phone was still lying on the dresser where I left it after Jewel hung up on me. If I grabbed it and called 9-1-1 I figured the cops would show up in time to find my dead body. If everything went well they'd even catch my killer and put him in jail, where he would come to see the error of his ways and take up crosswords or knitting, and be featured years later in a documentary about cons who had rediscovered their humanity in prison, and finally be released on parole and start a modestly successful store selling fashionable knitwear with a jailhouse swagger: but that would be cold comfort to me, wouldn't it? Because I'd be dead. I would be dead and my mom would come out to the cemetery every six months and stare bitterly at two graves instead of one.

Scritch, scratch. Scritch-scritch, scratch. The soft complaining creak of the metal window frame being quietly pried open. Then:

- soft thumping footsteps outside, someone running up, and
- muffled sounds of a struggle, and
- the damp smack of something hard clubbing into flesh
- a gasp, and
- people grappling outside my window in murderous silence, and
- a snap of bone breaking
- the faint ring and slash of metal, and
- a *spatter*, like raindrops hitting my window.

I threw myself out of bed and scrambled across the floor on my hands and knees, waiting for the window behind me to explode in a fountain of glass: waiting for bullet holes to open in my back.

I scuttled around the corner into the hallway.

- A heavy grunting *thump*, and
- bodies thudding into the side of the house.

Once in the hallway, out of the line of fire from the bedroom window, I got to my feet, a clumsy low crouch. I started to slap on the light switch but stopped because turning on the light would just make me easier to shoot. The fact that I knew the house in the dark was the only edge I had over whoever was trying to get in.

I ran to the bathroom and yanked open the make-up drawer, pawing through it in the dark, combs, my mother's hairbrush, hair ties, compact, lipsticks, and eyebrow pencils rattling around, crap I never wore anymore. Finally my hand found the little pair of scissors my Mom used to use to trim my Dad's eyebrows. I shut the bathroom door, locked it, and crept into the bathtub, quietly, quietly. I pulled the shower curtain closed, steel rings whispering and clinking along the rail as I crouched with my back under the shower head. I imagined a killer forcing the door—I would have to stab down with the scissors as hard as I could because I would only get one chance.

I stood there in the bathtub, my whole body shaking with fear, the little scissors like a toy in my hand. Waiting behind the locked door like Anne Frank in her attic, wondering if I was going to die.

Another thump, hard against the side of the house. A short bubbling shriek.

Silence.

Silence.

What the hell was going on out there?

7.